# THE RED CAR TO HOLLYWOOD

# THE RED CAR TO HOLLYWOOD

JENNIE LIU

THORNDIKE PRESS
A part of Gale, a Cengage Company

GALE
A Cengage Company


Image credits: metamorworks/Shutterstock (silhouette); STILLFX/Shutterstock; pashabo/Shutterstock; 100ker/Shutterstock; Cartone Animato/Shutterstock; -Slav-/Getty Images.
Thorndike Press, a part of Gale, a Cengage Company.


Thorndike Press® Youth Large Print Young Adult.
The text of this Large Print edition is unabridged.
Other aspects of the book may vary from the original edition.
Set in 16 pt. Plantin.

**LIBRARY OF CONGRESS CIP DATA ON FILE.**
**CATALOGUING IN PUBLICATION FOR THIS BOOK**
**IS AVAILABLE FROM THE LIBRARY OF CONGRESS.**

ISBN-13: 978-1-4205-3774-1 (hardcover alk. paper)

Published in 2026 by arrangement with Carolrhoda Lab®, an imprint of Lerner Publishing Group, Inc.

Print Number: 1 Print Year: 2026
Printed in Mexico

For Keira, Mei, Wilson, Riley, Shea,
and all the second-generationers.

**Note to readers:** Parts of this story deal with sexual violence.

## A NOTE ON TERMINOLOGY

Throughout *The Red Car to Hollywood*, characters use the term *Oriental* to refer to things and people from "the East" (with Europe, where the term originated, being the reference point). This was the common terminology of the period, and the characters in the novel use it as a neutral descriptive term, as would've been the convention then. Over time the word has developed racist connotations. In 1968, a student activist group at the University of California Berkeley sought to unite different ethnic groups of Asian descent into one organization, the Asian American Political Alliance, and the terms *Asian* and *Asian American* took root as preferred broad labels. In recent years, the limitations and breadth of *Asian American* continue to be explored.

The book's characters also use the terms *Negro,* in reference to Black Americans, and *American Indian*, in reference to Indigenous people and nations. Terminology has evolved since the 1920s and continues to do so. How people refer to themselves and how they prefer for others to refer to them can also vary from person to person.

# 1
## LOS ANGELES, MAY 1924

I was being watched.

I felt it like the crackling static of a wireless. Someone at the end of the shelves, fidgeting and staring. A cold prickle went up the back of my neck, but I resisted the urge to turn around. Instead, I propped my elbow on the reading table and buttressed my fingertips against my forehead to obscure my face. I was hiding out, skipping school, trying to act like I belonged here in the Central Public Library in the middle of the day. A college student maybe, studying art history and deeply immersed in *Chinese Art: Volume 2*.

But the prickles didn't go away. After a long minute, I closed the book and rose to return it to the shelf like any other ordinary patron.

I backed away, glowering at him, until I came to the end of the shelf and then spun on my heel. I went down the stairs with my head down and slipped past the charging desk, which swarmed with patrons clutching books and slips of paper. The library was housed in the top floors of the Metropolitan Building, but I avoided the elevators and took the stairs down the eight flights to ground level, ignoring the still-raw blisters on my feet.

After the marble and dark-wood coolness of the library, I was caught off guard by the bright sun as I burst outside. The stillness of the warm May air struck me in a strange way. It was only a couple of days since the winds had died down. Devil winds, Mr. Lew called them. That fumbling page had unnerved me, just as much as the ceaseless tattering of branches and the gusting winds that had howled in my ears as I'd trudged across the city that night. Was it just two days ago?

I squeezed my eyes to shut out the memory, then swept down the building's front steps. A brisk walk home would dispel the little pinpricks of unease at the edges of my mind.

Fifth Street wasn't nearly as busy as it had been in the morning, which oddly made me feel even more conspicuous on the sidewalk. With time to kill, I headed east, jigging my route so I could inspect different buildings and shop windows. I kept to the shade thrown by the store awnings, averting my eyes from the other pedestrians, but well aware of the glances thrown my way. Were they hostile? Leering?

I hated that the question even popped into my head. Why did I have to duck in the shadows when all I wanted to do was stroll down the sidewalk with the sun beaming fully on my face? I wanted to plant myself in front of each plate glass window to study the displays of merchandise like other girls did. But instead, with no more than fleeting glances, I scooted past polished wireless consoles, a flapper bride on the aisle of a faux church setting, and an Oldsmobile staged in the middle of a living room. I didn't stop because whenever I was outside Chinatown, I couldn't throw off that feeling that people were thinking, *What is she doing here?*

After six or seven blocks, the high-rise buildings became less imposing, less door and yanked it open. He turned his face away as if I wasn't even there. I forced myself to step inside. When he slammed the door behind me, the building shook so hard that plaster dust sifted down from the ceiling.

The knot inside me tightened as I moved to stand behind a tall yokeback chair.

Mrs. Kuen stood off to the side in front of a carved folding screen. She wasn't that old, but she always dressed in a no-fashion black smock dress that brushed her ankles. She was involved with the new Chinese Methodist Church, and she ran the Chinese Mission School where young Chinatown kids went after regular school to learn to read and write Chinese. She was considered the moral authority of the community.

When I nodded to her in greeting, she compressed her lips and looked at Ba.

My head filled with a white glare of dread as I waited for Ba to speak. His jaw was so tense that the muscles of his neck popped out like cords. He stared down at the floorboards, his lean frame bent, with a fist propped on a table as if he needed the support. We were several feet apart, but I could feel the anger radiating off him. Ma stood well back, leaning against a wardrobe, her eyes darting among the rest of us, with the pinch still between her brows.

Mrs. Kuen finally broke the strained silence and addressed me in Cantonese. "I was just telling your parents that I had a very distressing visit from Mrs. William Blythe."

Blood rushed to my face. It was worse than I'd thought. My hands curled around the slender wood of the chair's backrest.

"It seems that Mrs. Blythe is accusing you of . . ." Mrs. Kuen blinkered her eyelids and cleared a catch in her throat. "Well, she's accusing you of several things, including ensnaring her son Russell into a licentious relationship. And destruction of property."

Ma clamped her hand over her mouth. Ba closed his eyes and shook his head hard as if to shut out the words.

My brain hitched on the word *ensnared*. Ensnared! She made it sound like I was a crib girl calling out to men from behind a screen to draw them into a brothel. That was how the Blythes meant to paint me.

"It's not true." The blood in my head pounded against my temples. "It isn't! He . . . he . . ." The right word evaded my mind. *Courted? Wooed?* My knuckles were white from gripping the chair. It stuttered on its legs as I trembled. "He pursued me!" I was livid, too livid to be embarrassed about saying such things to Ba and Ma. And irrationally, I wanted to make it clear that Russell had chased me instead of the other way around.

They didn't care about that. I had associated with a boy — that was bad enough. But a white boy — unheard of. And people, his parents and Mrs. Kuen, had already begun to hear about it. A horrifying shame.

Mrs. Kuen puckered up her lips like she'd just tasted a sour plum. I could tell she didn't believe me. I opened my mouth to explain how Russell had waited for me that first day, but she stopped me cold.

"Mrs. Blythe is insisting on a payment of four hundred dollars for damages to the property."

"Four hundred dollars!" That was more than a month's worth of earnings from the store. I turned to Ba. "Ba, don't pay it! I didn't do anything!"

Ba closed his eyes. His nostrils flared wide. He wouldn't look at me.

"I didn't!"

Mrs. Kuen's gaze darted between Ba and me; she was plainly appalled that a girl would speak to her father like this. "Irene Blythe says she witnessed you and Russell in a . . ." The words died in her mouth, apparently too mortifying to say aloud.

"Russell and I . . . Yes, we were . . . *dating*," I stammered, flustered again at the wrong-sounding word. A foreign word, a foreign idea. At least to Ba and Ma.

Ma winced. Her other hand had made its way up to her face, and now both her hands mashed against her cheeks. Her eyes were bewildered, fixed on me as if she didn't know me.

My parents and I didn't discuss personal things — about feelings. They'd both been born in the old country. That set us worlds apart. Ba rarely addressed me unless it had to do with work needing to be done for the store. But even Ma and

Mrs. Kuen and Ma both jumped. Ma clutched at the fabric of her housedress.

For the next minute, Ba's breathing was the only sound in the room. He stared out the storefront windows. Finally, he straightened up, tugging at the hem of his waistcoat as he stepped toward the door.

"I'll come to see you tomorrow. We'll certainly sort this out before I leave for my buying trip later this month." Ba opened the door for Mrs. Kuen. It was her cue to leave.

After he closed the door behind her, Ba leaned his forehead against the glass. My breath was stuck in my throat. Now that Mrs. Kuen was gone, I steeled myself for Ba's apoplectic rage. My impulse was to badger him not to pay. To plead, to argue, anything to fill up the awful silence and release the agitation building in me. But I kept quiet.

Ba had never whipped me, but I'd also never done anything like this. A queasy feeling came over me. What if he demanded to know everything that had gone on between Russell and me? My ears turned hot. A beating would be easier to take.

Ba's eyes finally lit on me. Another long moment passed. Then he grabbed the celadon bowl from the table and launched it across the room. Ma cried out, and I jumped as it crashed against the wall.

"Get upstairs!" Ba roared at me. "You go upstairs, and you stay there!"

I crossed the room, hurrying toward our living quarters, my shoes crunching against the pale green shards.

# 2

## MARCH 1924

The funny thing was that Mrs. Kuen was the one who'd inadvertently connected Russell and me when she arranged my piano lessons with his sister Irene.

We had moved to Los Angeles from San Francisco in late February, when Ba took a partnership with Mr. Lew. A couple of weeks after we settled in, Mrs. Kuen visited Ma to invite us to the Chinese Methodist Church. Ma led her upstairs to our sitting room. Perched on our worn velveteen sofa, Mrs. Kuen let her eyes wander over the altar table with the brass incense burner, the red scrolls that recorded our ancestors' names, Ba's rocking chair with the padded leather seat, and Ma's embroidery loom resting on a worktable. I was more than a little proud of our mix of secondhand American furniture and marred Chinese pieces from the shop, proud that

Ba had been successful enough to move us beyond a single crowded room.

When Mrs. Kuen spotted our small piano and asked who played, Ma told her that I was self-taught. Mrs. Kuen asked me to play for her, so I sat down and pounded out "Everyone Loves My Baby," or at least my best rendition of it. I'd heard the song often back in San Francisco at my friend Mary's place. Her family owned a big shirt factory and had a Radiola.

Mrs. Kuen's mouth twitched. I couldn't tell what displeased her more: the loud, jazzy tune, or the dropped notes from the broken or out-of-tune keys. She mentioned that the church was saving up for a piano and suggested that I learn to read music so I could play at services. She had associations with another church, First Methodist, and knew of a girl from that congregation who gave lessons.

Although the prospect of playing hymns in church didn't particularly excite me, I agreed, hoping at least I could make some friends that way. Our move to Los Angeles had been a big letdown. Chinatown in San Francisco had been like its own city. We'd rarely needed to venture beyond the

Angeles in an intricate network, and then there were Red Cars that went out beyond the city. In this one way, Los Angeles was more impressive than San Francisco.

Irene, the piano teacher Mrs. Kuen had recommended, turned out to be twenty-two — hardly a girl — and white. At first, I was guarded, seeing as how I'd been ignored and condescended to by the white girls at my new school. But Irene was puppy-dog friendly. Right away, she pulled me onto the bench to sit next to her and started chattering to me.

I was two or three lessons in when Russell showed up one afternoon. Irene and I were seated at the piano. She plinked out a hymn, naming each note as she played. This, she said, would cement them in my head. I nodded along at each tap of the keys, though inwardly I sighed, wondering why I needed to know the names of the notes. It seemed easier to run my fingers up and down the keys following the rise and fall of the notes on the page.

I caught sight of Russell, leaning against a doorframe on the side of the sanctuary. He wore a gray belted suit and held a large picnic basket with both hands. Irene had mentioned that she had a date with her fiancé following the lesson — a sunset picnic in the hills — and that her brother was to bring the food sent by their mother.

I dipped my head and may not have taken any more notice of him except that his eyes fixed on me in the most intense way, and a smile played on his lips. He nodded back, and the light streaming in from the stained glass window glinted gold on his slicked-back tawny hair. I was suddenly conscious that my own locks were splayed messily down my back, but I resisted the itch to gather them and rake them smooth. I turned back to the sheet music.

Irene completed her demonstration, then spotted her brother. "Russell!" She jumped up, her coppery curls bouncing, and ran over to take the basket. "Thank you, thank you! You're a doll! Let's see what Mama packed for me."

"Well, what Lucille packed for you anyway," Russell said.

Irene wrinkled her nose at being corrected. "Lucille's our housekeeper and cook," she explained to me. She flipped the lid up and went into raptures about the fried chicken and potato salad.

"I guess I'll start for home." I stood up and edged out from behind the bench.

"But we still have fifteen minutes!" Irene said. "Pierre won't be coming by before then anyway. Let me just put this over here." She set the picnic hamper on a pew and urged me to sit down.

I started playing and tried to concentrate on reading the notes aloud as I struck the keys. From the corner of my eye, I saw that Russell watched me for another minute before he slipped out the door.

Twenty minutes later, I exited the church. Two huge eucalyptus trees scented the air and cast shade against the flat blue sky. I hadn't gone but a few yards past the scrolled iron gates when I noticed Russell half a block ahead. He leaned against a black Ford Model T with his ankles crossed.

Our eyes met, and he straightened up. I almost stopped in my tracks as the realization sprang to my mind: he was waiting for me.

I recovered my step, hoping he hadn't noticed the hesitation. As I neared him, he moved into the center of the sidewalk.

"Hi," he said.

I had to stop then.

"All done in there?"

I inclined my head.

"I'm Russell Blythe, by the way. My rude sister didn't introduce us."

"Rude? I think she's awfully nice. I'm Ruby Chan."

"You go to Polytech High, don't you? I've seen you on campus."

He'd noticed me. I couldn't keep the surprise off my face. Polytech was huge compared to my school in San Francisco. "I'm a junior."

"Senior here," Russell said. "You're new this year."

I nodded again. An awkward silence fell between us, which was strange. I wasn't usually shy. In the store, I prided myself on being able to talk up a customer until I figured out what they liked and what they didn't know they needed. But Russell was no lady browsing vases for her mantel, and I wasn't used to this kind of attention from a boy. A white boy.

Russell didn't seem uncomfortable, but the way he looked at me made the backs of my knees soft.

"Well, listen," I said, one side of my mouth turning up into a smile. "I've got to catch my streetcar."

"Where're you going? Home? I can give you a ride. You live in Chinatown?"

"Yes," I answered but then quickly added, "I mean, yes, I live in Chinatown, but no, I don't need a ride." Ba would be more than shocked if I rode up in a vehicle with a boy, any boy, and a white one would be unthinkable. "I have to hurry. I see the streetcar coming. Nice meeting you."

"Nice meeting you," Russell echoed as I passed him.

I felt his eyes on me as I moved down the sidewalk toward the Yellow Car stop. I tried to walk normally despite the thrill that ran down my spine.

On the streetcar I sank into a seat. A young boy wearing a newsboy cap twisted around and stared at me with an unsmiling look. I turned away. The windows weren't glassed in at the rear of the streetcar, and the wind cooled my face as we screeched and clanged through streets teeming with motorcars and pedestrians. The buildings rolled by as I pulled my hair around and combed my fingers through it, wondering at the peculiar little encounter with Russell. I can't say I didn't like the way he'd looked at me. Everything suddenly felt different.

A persistent *bleep, bleep, bleep* rose over the rattle of traffic. I leaned out the window and scanned the congested street behind us. Vehicles swerved around each other and around the streetcars that ran down the center of the road. A few vehicles back, an arm flew out from a driver's side window and waved wildly. Then a head poked out. It was Russell.

He grinned at me before he ducked back into his car. The black Ford bucked and darted around the other automobiles until it was alongside the streetcar. Russell stretched out the window again, and his eyes locked on me.

"Ruby Chan!" he hollered. "I *will* be seeing you!"

There was a collective tittering in the streetcar as Russell bleated his horn a few more times. The woman in front of me twisted around with a scandalized expression. I ignored her and tracked the Ford as it wove through the traffic, my heart galloping in my chest. I was sure its jumping was visible through my blouse, because the boy in the cap gawped at me with out-and-out wonderment. I smiled at him until his mother told him to turn around.

# 3

## MAY 1924

A week after Mrs. Kuen delivered the slanderous report about me, Ma pushed me out the back door with a basket of laundry as bulky as one of the carved rosewood trunks Ba sold in the store. It was heavy, and I bumped against the doorframe, scraping my knuckles on the splintered wood.

I scowled. Taking the wash down the street to Quon's laundry was usually my younger brothers' job, but extra chores were part of my punishment. I tightened my grip on the handles and started lugging the basket down the narrow alley.

"Take it to Sam Kee Laundry," Ma called out in an urgent tone.

I twisted around. "Sam Kee?"

"It's over on North Figueroa."

Joe, since they'd be home from school in a little while. I supposed she didn't think it was healthy for me to be shut in completely. She'd probably sent me all the way over to North Figueroa Street to give me a little more time away from those suffocating rooms doing those suffocating tasks. I blessed her for that. And I didn't want to make her regret the gesture by staying out too long.

So as much as I wanted to watch the rest of the filming, I picked up my basket and hurried on.

Sam Kee Laundry was easy to locate because of the signboard that spanned the upper half of the two-story clapboard building. It stood alone, unattached to any other structure. A makeshift staircase at the side went up to the flat roof, where sheets and men's shirts were hanging from lines strung on posts.

The door was propped open, and the humid air and the scent of lye hit me even before I entered the cramped space of the service room. I expected to see someone like Mr. Quon manning the counter, but a young woman was perched on a tall stool behind it, idly fiddling with an abacus. Her eyes were on the beads, but I only had to see the long fan of her lashes, the thin arc of brows, and the straight-across cut of her bangs to realize that I recognized her.

It was Anna May Wong, the moving-picture actress.

The *Chinese* moving-picture actress.

I knew her father was a laundryman. Everyone knew it, because the picture magazines liked to mention that, but I hadn't come across the family's store until now.

Thanks to the movie magazines, I also knew that Anna May was nineteen, just three years older than me. I had seen her on the screen playing the jilted Chinese lover of a white man in *The Toll of the Sea*, and it was hard to believe she'd been only sixteen when she filmed it. Now, in her middy blouse with the sailor bow tie, she still looked like a high school girl.

Another woman — white, with short dark hair capped by a green cloche — leaned against a worktable wedged into the other half of the room. She held a notepad near her face, tilting it toward the window and counting the pieces. I gazed at her, trying to align the tragic, lovesick woman I'd seen on the big screen with this girl, dewy-faced from the humid air of wash vats and irons, pawing through my family's sheets. Just like that, she was another Chinese daughter working at her father's business. I almost laughed at the absurdity of it.

Anna May glanced up at me. "What is it?"

I shook my head.

"I can tell you're hiding a smile." A smirk showed at one end of her lip.

"Oh, just the *good Chinese daughter* thing." I mimed the reporter's self-satisfied tone and fanned myself with an imaginary notebook.

Anna May laughed. "Let her think what she wants. Maybe she'll write it up that way. It makes a nice story." She slid the sheets into a basket she pulled up from behind the counter. "I haven't seen you around before. What's your name?"

"Ruby Chan. We moved here a few months ago from San Francisco."

"Ah! You're most welcome to LA. There're so few girls our age here — I mean a teeny, tiny population — so a new face is really refreshing. You go to Lincoln High? Why aren't you in school today?"

"Polytech, actually." I ignored the second question. The truth was that I was finished with school. I was never going back. Even though Ba had insisted I stay at home since Mrs. Kuen's visit, I'd already stopped going to school two days before that, because I couldn't bear to see *him*.

Besides, I didn't need school. I would've graduated in another year, but by now I'd learned everything that would help me run the store with Ba, which was what I'd decided to do. I was already helping keep the books, and as for the rest — the ins and outs of hunting quality pieces, merchandising, and display — I'd learn all that from Ba and Mr. Lew. I'd been readying my counterargument for when Ba got over being furious and decided it was time for me to return to my classes.

I changed the subject. "They're filming something now down at the Plaza. It seems to be a comedy."

at all intimidating like you'd expect of an actress. As I picked up the ticket, I wondered if we could be friends. I certainly could use one now.

# 4

Just as I passed by the Plaza on my way home, the yellow Packard from the filming roared by, swirling up a huge cloud of dust that settled on the spectators. I caught a glimpse of the movie players in the front seat — the flapper clutching her hat against her head and the fella with his head tossed back, laughing as he gripped the wheel.

The camera was being loaded into a truck, and I dawdled to watch, but soon it was gone and then there was nothing more to see.

At the corner of my street, I decided to peek through our shop windows before I went in through the back, just to get a hint of how business was going.

In the months since we'd arrived, Ba had taken inventory, cleaned and polished every item, and done everything he could think of to turn the store around. Still, sales hadn't improved much.

The thought of the four hundred dollars the Blythes had demanded stuck me like a hot poker. I hoped Ba hadn't paid. I just wanted to forget Russell, forget that any of this had happened.

To my surprise, the CLOSED sign hung in the door's window. I peered through the glass and scanned the cluttered shop. No one was inside. Ba never closed the shop this early. Had someone fallen ill? Was Mrs. Kuen back?

I hurried around to the alley and into the back room, which was both a storage area for the store and our kitchen. Ba, Ma, and a woman I'd never seen before sat at the table in front of the cookstove. They all turned to me with startled expressions.

"The CLOSED sign is up in the window." I pressed a hand to my chest. "I thought something might've happened." My eyes drifted to the woman, who wore a plain indigo tunic with knots, her graying hair drawn back in a tight bun.

The auntie's eyes roved over me in turn. I was a mess, sweaty and flushed. The tie of my hair had slipped down again, and I could feel strands sticking to my neck. Ma rose, moved beside me, and began smoothing my hair.

Ba's expression darkened. "Where have you been? You're supposed to be upstairs." There was anger in his voice, although I knew he was trying to stay calm because of his guest.

"She was dropping off the laundry," Ma said in her soothing murmur. "I sent her out with it." She turned to me. "Now, upstairs. Work on your embroidery. I'll call you when we're done here so you can begin supper preparations." She placed her hands on my shoulders and squeezed like she used to whenever I was too noisy or overexcited as a child.

I moved around some crates and broken furniture and started up the stairs. They were all watching me, especially the auntie. Once I was at the top of the steps, out of sight, Ba picked up the conversation.

"She's making the most exquisite pillow casing in the Shu embroidery technique," he said.

I paused, confused at the word choice. Ba had insisted that Ma teach me embroidery, and I was working on a pillow casing, but *exquisite* wouldn't be how I described my needlework. Frankly, my skill level was about that of a five-year-old.

"And a coverlet too — so many rich colors," Ba added.

He was talking about Ma's work, not mine. She was close to finishing the coverlet, which she'd been working on for more than a year. I'd noticed she had stepped up her work on it this week as she supervised my housework and needlework lessons.

"The two silvery cranes sparkle against the clouds. So many shades of blue and gray, it almost seems painted! Her skill is most extraordinary." I was pleased to hear Ba boast about Ma's needlework. Was he already trying to sell it?

The auntie's unfamiliar voice floated up. "Ah, cranes for a long married life! A wedding piece! I'd like to see it. Why don't you have the girl bring them down?"

Ba coughed. "Perhaps on your next visit." I could hear the unease in his voice. "She's very modest about showing unfinished work."

"Silk embroidery is a fine hobby for girls these days," said the auntie. "So many of them don't want to take the time to learn the art. And she's a good cook?"

Alarm bells were going off in my head.

"Yes! She does all the cooking for the family, the cleaning, as well as taking care of her brothers."

"And pretty too!" The auntie chuckled. "Not that beauty matters too much when there are so few women to be had."

I thought of how the auntie had eyed me like she was choosing a melon from a produce cart. A cold tingle ran up my spine.

I heard the scraping of stools against the floorboards. They were getting up.

"I'll be taking the train back to San Francisco tomorrow," the auntie was saying. "It may take a few weeks to find the best match . . ."

I gripped the banister. She was a matchmaker.

"There's no hurry, no hurry," Ma said.

"The sooner the better," Ba contradicted her. "Though a good bride price would be most welcome."

They were trying to marry me off. All week I'd been getting a speed course in high domesticity. Ma had taken me in hand, pushing me to cook more complicated dishes, coaching me through the advanced sewing techniques that were second nature to her. They had been planning this.

I wanted to charge downstairs and make a scene — show myself to be rough and uncivil, the complete opposite of the cultured and obedient housewife that Ba aimed to portray. But the shock of it all held me back.

"We won't make any decisions until you get back from your trip," Ma said with a supplicating note to her words. I assumed she was speaking to Ba, since he was due to leave for China next Saturday.

"Have a photograph taken of her and send copies to me as soon as you can," the matchmaker said. "That'll help a great deal with getting good offers."

The soft tinkle of the bell from the shop door floated up as the auntie left. I ran down the stairs and into the store before the door had even fully closed.

"A matchmaker!"

Ba spun around with the OPEN/CLOSED sign still in his hand.

"Why are you talking to a matchmaker?!"

He squinted at me, nostrils flaring. I flinched and immediately regretted my outburst.

Ba's face was set. "Time to get married."

My mouth went dry. "Oh, no." I shook my head. "No!"

Who even thinks about getting married? Certainly not me. And not like this — with a matchmaker involved. Ba and Ma had been married by an arrangement of some sort, and I knew it still happened. Plenty of Chinese parents thought they owned your body. But I'd been born *here*. I knew of a few older girls back in San Francisco who'd been married by arrangement, the brides' and grooms' photos exchanged by parents. These days, though, just as many girls chose their own husbands. With their parents' approval, of course.

Marriage to a stranger was incomprehensible. Ba couldn't be serious.

I wheeled around to look at Ma. She clasped her hands and brought them to her chin. Her face was full of angst, but she didn't say anything. Of course, she never went against Ba.

threshold, swatting at their clothes. To me, she said, "Take their bags back and get them some bao to eat on their way to Chinese school."

I picked up their bags and went to get the buns, my head throbbing from the cut-off argument with Ba. It wasn't enough to squirrel me away in the house. He wanted to permanently stopper any possible gossip by sending me away to a husband. Possibly as far away as China! I still couldn't believe it.

Once I returned with the bao and passed them to the boys, they scurried off to their Chinese lessons with Mrs. Kuen.

"Ma, please —" I started, but she put her hand up.

"Let's work on dinner." Her face was weary as she edged past me.

In the back room, she tucked a few wayward strands into the hair bun at her nape and tied an apron over her housedress. She swept the tea things off the table. "Put on your apron and get the meat."

I pulled a chunk of pork out of the icebox. Ma had shown me how to marinate it with soya, garlic, and fermented black bean.

"Put it on that board and sliver it," she said.

I scowled as I dropped the slab of meat on the board and began sawing at it with a cleaver.

Ma *tsk*ed. "Not like that." She left the cups in the sink and wiped her hands on a cloth. "Let me show you." Taking the knife out of my hand, she began slicing the meat in strips as thin as matchsticks. "Now you try." She handed the cleaver back to me.

I wanted to hack at the meat, but I tried to do it like she showed me. The pulsing in my head was beginning to subside. Ma watched me slice several pieces before I said, "Ba can't be serious about the matchmaker."

Ma went back to the cups, pumping the faucet to get the water going. The small window over the sink lit her face. "Your ba and I had a blind marriage. I was sixteen when I was married." Her face pinked and she clamped her lips into a thin line.

I knew then that she wasn't entirely committed to marrying me off. This was all Ba. "But that was almost twenty years ago. Things are different now!"

Ma never talked much about her past. Everything I knew about it I had overheard over the years in San Francisco, when she talked with the aunties who visited on occasion to do needlework and drink tea. I'd gleaned that Ma had been born in China and had been sold as a child to work as a servant to a wealthy Chinese family. When the family had emigrated to America, they'd claimed her as a daughter to get her into the country. Not long afterward, she'd married Ba.

"Can't you talk to Ba?" I knew it would be hard for her, but she was my only hope. She didn't want this for me, I could see that much. "He has to know I'm not ready for marriage. He's only doing this to punish me —"

"Ruby-ah." Ma hung her head. Her hands were still in the sink, but she had stopped washing. "You've gone too far. Even to be out with a boy, a Chinese boy, can ruin the chance of a good man marrying you."

"But I don't care about getting married!"

She slapped the edge of the sink with her fingertips. "You have to care!" She closed her eyes. "Ba's right. I've not trained you well enough. Somehow, I've permitted disobedience in our house."

I drew in my lip and turned back to slicing the pork. I was sorry that Ma blamed herself — that Ba blamed her — but I didn't know what to say. Everything was so confused.

"What about the laundry? When will it be ready?" The hushed urgency crept into her voice again, and the change of subject was so abrupt that I twisted around. Ma kept her eyes fixed on the dishes in the sink.

"Couple of days," I said. "Why did you ask me about James Wong earlier? Is he the proprietor of the laundry?"

She glanced at the short passage that led to the shop. It was still quiet in the store. Ba still had not come inside. "No, he's the oldest boy. About your age. Graduating high school this month." She gave me a pointed look.

The cleaver slowed in my hand as I tried to work out what she was getting at.

"He's very handsome. Grew up so much like you. American born. Second-generation, maybe third. And their family" — her

# 6

The rest of the evening passed with a heavy silence among Ma, Ba, and me. At the dinner table, I threw dark looks at Ba over the greens, bitter melon, and pork Ma pushed at me, but he avoided my gaze and kept his eyes moodily on his plate.

Danny and Joe chattered, quibbled, and stuffed their mouths, oblivious to the tension in the air. We finished eating and cleaned up. Ma went upstairs to work on the coverlet. I sat with the boys at the table, supposedly helping them with their math, but really I ignored them while I stewed and bit on a thumbnail.

I seethed, but a cold needle of fear was there too. How does a girl defy her parents? Would I have to run away? Where would I go? I had no money for a room, no job. I had experience working in the store, but would anyone else hire me? The Chinese community was too close-knit, so I couldn't stay in the neighborhood.

I thought about all the businesses downtown — drugstores, movie houses, even factories. When we moved here, especially after I met Russell, my world had expanded beyond Chinatown. But now I knew that I'd merely been a visitor in the shadows.

Did I dare try to get a job out there? Or could I go back to San Francisco? Would my old friends take me in? Despite our promises to write, I'd quickly lost touch with even my best pals, Mary and Lillie. If I showed up at either of their doors, they would surely let me in, but their parents would be quick to send me home.

When their homework was done, the boys and I trooped upstairs. I wedged myself between them on the sofa and read to them from *Treasure Island*. The sentences tumbled out of my mouth, but the story circumvented my brain.

Ba came up with the inventory ledger and a clipboard and settled in his chair beneath the gas lamp on the wall. I had always considered Ba to be forward-thinking.

His western suits, the Brilliantine in his hair, his buying the shop and letting me learn from Mr. Lew had all given me that impression.

I remembered how he'd let me sit behind the counter as he spoke with customers at the shops where he worked in San Francisco. How I'd stood by his shoulder when he did the books or checked the inventory. He used to absentmindedly talk out loud as he wrote down descriptions of the objects. When I'd started asking questions, he'd always taken the time to explain the workings of the shop.

But now I realized that he was still very much of the old world. I had been an immoral girl. I was willful. He thought it was completely rational to tether me to some man before my wicked acts came to light.

He lit a cigar and began to study the ledgers. I saw now that it'd been stupid to challenge him earlier. Showing my temper had only made him more determined, and the stubborn clench of his jaw hadn't relaxed. The urge to bring it all up again bubbled inside me, but I warned myself it wasn't the right time, since my last angry words were still hot on my tongue.

Though I tried to concentrate on *Treasure Island*, I was distracted by Ba flipping the pages of the ledger and scratching with his pencil at the page on the clipboard. I knew that was the list of items he wanted to purchase while he was in China.

"Ba, I know you'll be sure to get more porcelain," I said. "Chinese customers like the blue and white pieces, and the wucai ones seem to draw in the white ladies." I didn't have to mention that the white ladies always had more money to spend. Once they made up their mind to purchase some porcelain, they could often be drawn into buying a teak chair or some other expensive piece of furniture.

Ba peered at me over his frameless glasses. The expression on his face didn't change, but after a moment he gave a miniscule nod and went back to writing.

Emboldened, I closed the book, marking the place with my hand.

"Sissy! Don't stop there!" The boys whined and pulled on my arms.

I put my hand up for them to hush. "And I'm sure you'll collect as many lacquer pieces as you can, Ba. Small everyday things are good, but furniture too, like those cabinets with painted enamel designs or mother-of-pearl inlays." I thought about the ladies featured in magazines wearing sequined dresses and feather boas, the yellow Packard on the movie set earlier today, the patterned velvet and scrolled-arm furniture in the department store windows. I scooted to the edge of the sofa cushion. "Everything is so showy these days. Maybe we could get one of those carved red lacquered canopy beds and have it as a centerpiece against one wall of the store. We could dress it with silk bedding . . ."

Ba pulled the cigar from his mouth and ground it out in the ashtray on the little table next to his chair. Lines of annoyance marked his forehead. The ideas were good, and we both knew it, but I was pushing my luck. Again.

Before Ba could respond, Ma carefully set aside her embroidery and stood up. "Come on — bedtime. Everyone!"

The boys grumbled but went downstairs with Ma and Ba to wash up, while I cleaned out Ba's ashtray and pulled my nightgown from the chifforobe. I couldn't change until the others were already in bed because Ba thought it indecorous for anyone to see me in my nightclothes.

When it was my turn to use the toilet, I went down. By the time I returned, everyone had gone into their rooms. My bed was in the corner of the sitting room behind a mended tri-fold silk screen. I turned off the gas in the lamp, slipped behind the screen, and climbed onto my cot.

I lay there unable to sleep, my mind going round and round. Marriage. It was unimaginable. Even Ma's notion for me to get to know James Wong, who might be young and as attractive as Anna May, felt so wrong.

When Ma said the family might be *accustomed to understanding trouble*, what she meant was what the rest of the Chinese community thought — that Anna May, *that daughter who plays in the moving pictures*, was a scandal. I supposed Ma thought that if my disgrace came out, the

Wong family might still accept me. Maybe Ma meant well, but the whole idea struck me as disturbing. As if I was a liability to be dealt with.

Faint moonlight glowed through the muslin curtains at the open window near the foot of the bed. My thoughts reeled back to that afternoon in Hollywoodland with Russell, how sunlight had streamed in through the windows of Irene's nearly completed house. I put my hands to my face and scrubbed them against my cheeks, trying to rub out the memories. A fierce rush of longing blew through me. Despite everything that had happened.

I tossed back the sheets, crawled to the window, and pushed aside the curtains. The half-moon hung in the sky, stars dotting the inky blackness. There was no one out on the street below, and all the windows were dark except for one at the far end of the street, which I knew to be a gambling den. The faint sputter of a motorcar came from down the street, and a few minutes later a train on Alameda rattled on the rails as it headed to the railyard just beyond Chinatown.

The noises only made me remember more: the times I'd been out there, feeling unfettered in the city that was mine as much as anyone else's. How I'd slipped downstairs and stolen out into the blustery dark that night.

I shuddered, desire and contempt all confused. I hated to admit how I longed for him. Even now.

# 7

## MARCH - APRIL 1924

I will *be seeing you!*

After that Wednesday when Russell chased my trolley, instead of ducking my head and making a beeline for my classrooms at school, I found myself dawdling in the hallways, scanning the hordes of students for his honey-brown head.

I spotted him two days later as I was eating lunch under a jacaranda tree. I had planted myself there for the clear view of the double doors at the front entrance and was rewarded when he burst out of the building with a bunch of other boys. They loitered under the portico at the top of the wide steps. The sky was cracking blue, and the guys had their jackets slung over their shoulders as they laughed and threw fake punches at one another.

Sitting alone with my knees tucked to the side, I felt a wave of self-consciousness come over me. So I busied myself with packing up the remains of my peanut butter sandwich. From the tail of my eye, I saw Russell survey the grounds. For a moment, I thought he saw me, but when I raised my head, hoping he would come over and talk to me, he nudged one of the fellas beside him, and they all strolled down the stairs and went the other way.

Still, the following Wednesday after my piano lesson, he was waiting for me in the same crossed-ankles position, leaning against his car with his hands in his pockets. My pulse began to race, but my step didn't falter this time, even as he watched me with a small smile on his lips.

"Hi, Ruby."

I stopped beside him, clutching my schoolbooks low against my stomach. "Hi, Russell."

"How was your lesson?"

"Oh, it was dandy," I said lightly, although inside my nerves were thrumming.

"You have 'Jesus Loves Me' down tight?" Russell asked.

I flipped my braid over my shoulder. "Oh, yes. As good as 'All Things Bright and Beautiful.'"

We both laughed. Russell's chuckle was low, soft. My own was high-toned and full of nervous energy. He was flirting with me. And I was flirting back. *Flirting!*

I ducked my head and rocked on my heels, then said, "Well, I'd better go."

Russell pushed up off the Ford and opened the passenger door. "How about a ride?"

I was so tempted to say yes, but I shook my head. I meant to leave it at that, but impulsively I said, "Not today." The slightest opening for him to ask me again.

"Okay then." His tone lilted up and he grinned. He started to move to his car, but then he spun around. "Let's go to the pictures sometime? Next week! I'll scoop you up after school."

I laughed at his eagerness and found myself saying, "All right, let's do it" — with no thought to the rules: that a Chinese girl should never be with a boy on her own; that the Chinese and the white shouldn't mix. Particularly when it came to dating.

■■■■

The next Wednesday on the way to school, I slipped into Guthrie Drugs and dropped my streetcar fare into a coin-operated phone at the back of the store. I dialed the number Russell had given me and left a message for Irene that I'd be missing our piano lesson that afternoon. I had to skip it, because to do both the lesson and the picture would get me home so late that Ma and Ba would demand to know where I'd been.

After school, Russell was waiting for me on a corner a block away. He drove us to a small movie house on South Broadway. Judging by the cracked glass of the ticket booth and the sticky floor, the place had seen better days, but I was glad he hadn't chosen a theater too close to Chinatown where we might be spotted by someone from the neighborhood. A handful of people were scattered in the seats — some kids who appeared to be high school or college students, a few down-on-their-luck men, and a couple of women who must not have had kids to worry about. Russell moved toward the back row.

"Where are you going?" I caught him by the cuff of his jacket. "Let's sit down at the front."

"Really?" He made a face.

"Yes! The screen's so big from there. The music too." I gestured at the upright piano stationed off to the side of the screen.

Russell sighed and turned his palm up for me to lead the way. We settled into the very first row as the lights went out.

Russell laid his arm on the armrest between us and leaned closer to me. "These seats are great." His breath was warm in my ear, his tone good-natured.

The film started, but my enthusiasm for the close-up movie experience shifted to Russell. The flickering light from the screen bounced off his face. My shoulder and arm pressed against him. I wondered if he'd wanted to sit in the back so we could kiss. Heat bloomed inside me — from embarrassment at being so naïve, but also from desire.

It was almost impossible for me to focus on the picture, a comedy called *Girl Shy* about a self-conscious fella who was struggling to win a girl despite having written a book about how to get girls. The piano player was making an awful racket, pounding out low, somber notes that didn't fit the mood of the film at all. He was almost falling off the bench. Some guys sitting halfway up the back booed him.

Russell nudged me and pointed at the piano player. "He must be drunk."

I didn't doubt it. Although Prohibition was in full swing, I knew people could still get ahold of liquor. I'd even seen Ba downing a few shots with his friends at the New Year banquets.

A crushed popcorn box sailed across the room and hit the piano player on the shoulder. The music crashed to a stop and he turned a befuddled glare toward the audience. The guttering light from the silent screen flashed over him as he rose unsteadily to his feet.

"Hey, hey, who did tha'?" he slurred. "Why would you do tha'?" He squinted into the dark room, swaying as he tried to step around the bench, but he tripped and fell to his knees.

Russell muffled a laugh. I elbowed him and jumped up to help the fella. Russell got up as well, and together we got him

the ticket. "Gosh, I'm such a sap. I left it at home."

"Uh-oh." He turned up his hands. "No ticket, no wash."

A groan slipped out of my mouth. I was about to beg him to make an exception, but he held up his hand and grinned.

"I'm kidding. Just don't tell my pop. What's the name?"

I ducked my head gratefully, relieved that I didn't have to run all the way home. "Chan. Ruby Chan."

He smiled before he turned away from the counter. "James Wong, at your service."

I watched him pick through the brown paper packets on the shelf behind him. His shoulders were broad, and his shirt and braces strained against his shoulder blades. I found myself wondering if he boxed or played baseball. Definitely some sport. He pulled down several bundles and plopped them into my basket. "That's a heavy load you have there."

"I can handle it." As I paid for the laundry, I heard the quick, sharp sound of shoes approaching from the workroom.

Anna May strode into the service area, sporting a turquoise linen blouse with wide-cut sleeves and a close-fitting hat with an arching brim. The outfit was smart and fashionable, so different from what she'd worn the other day — the good Chinese daughter, the schoolgirl, left in the dust.

"Jimmy, Papa said he can spare you for an hour. He's coming out to —" She caught sight of me, and her face brightened. "Ruby! You made it back. It's swell to see you."

"I was hoping to run into you." I grinned. "I mean, we had such a nice talk the other day."

"We did. And I wish I had time to chew the fat again, but my brother and I are going out to buy a typewriter." She turned to him. "Papa's coming down now to take over the counter, so let's blow this joint."

James started rolling down his sleeves.

I pulled the basket off the counter. "Well, maybe I'll catch you next time."

Anna May grabbed a vest and a suit jacket from a hook on the wall and chucked them onto the counter for James. "Hey, why don't you come with us?" she said to me. "A trip downtown is always fun."

The invitation was so unexpected that I blinked at her, tongue-tied, then glanced at James. He lifted his brows as he pulled on his vest, as if to second the invitation.

I wanted to go. Of course I wanted to, but the laundry basket was dead weight in my arms. "I wish I could" — I joggled the basket — "but I've got to get this home."

Anna May waved her hand, flinging aside my excuse. "Leave it here for now. You can take it after we get back."

"That's a fine idea!" Ba stayed in the store all morning and would be distracted with final preparations for his trip; he wouldn't notice that I wasn't around. If he did, Ma would surely cover for me. Ma wouldn't mind, would she? I'd be doing exactly what she wanted: spending time with James Wong, getting to know him. The notion made me squirm a little, but then I pictured going home to our airless rooms. Scrubbing floors. Beating rugs.

James put on his jacket and settled a cap over his head. He and Anna May were both utterly snazzy compared to me in my low-sashed dress and thin cotton stockings. Ma made most of our clothes and did keep me up with the fashion to a certain extent. The shape was always in style, but she kept the frills to a minimum.

Anna May poked her head back into the workroom and yelled, "Papa, we're leaving!"

We hustled over to Spring and Temple and jumped on a Yellow Car to the shopping district. James, sitting in front of Anna May and me, was quiet at first. I was too, feeling strangely reserved.

"Ruby goes to Polytech," Anna May told James.

"Oh yeah?" James shifted in his seat so he could look back at us. "I'm at Lincoln."

"How do you like it?" I asked.

"It's fine. But I can't wait to shove off to USC next year."

"Hence the typewriter," Anna May said. "My little graduation gift for him."

"I'd be happier if you bought me a motorcar. I'd even let you drive it, if you promised you wouldn't crash it like you did your little roadster."

"Grrr!" Anna May squinted at him playfully. "You hush up!"

"Where are we going?" I asked, putting on a casual tone.

"Blythe's," Anna May answered.

My stomach dropped to my feet.

Blythe's Department Store was owned by Russell's family. They were in and out of the store all the time. In fact, the one time I'd gone there out of curiosity, I'd spotted Irene and an older woman, swishing down the aisle with shopping bags laced on their arms. I'd darted behind a stand of mannequins.

"Does . . . does Blythe's even have typewriters?" I stammered.

"Sure they do," James said. "My buddy Tommy got one there last week. Said they were having a sale on them."

Anna May steered us along the crowded sidewalk toward the four-story building. I couldn't show my face in that store. His parents wouldn't know me, but what if I ran into Russell himself? Or worse, Irene. Her horrified expression from that awful afternoon sprang into my mind.

"What about going to Formann's? It's huge." My throat was dry and tight. "I'll bet they have a bigger selection."

"Mm, since we're right here we might as well go in." James reached for the gold handle on the glass door.

"You two go ahead," I said, hanging back as Anna May moved toward the door. "I think I'll wait out here and . . . look at the window displays."

"What?" Anna May turned back and peered at me from under the brim of her hat. "That's silly. Don't you want to see at all the pretty, shiny things inside?"

"If you don't want to look at typewriters, you can look at . . ." James faltered for a second. "Shoes, or hats, or something."

"You know what? I think I'm going to run over to Formann's. I heard they did an expansion last year and the store runs the whole block now." Russell had told me that.

Anna May was studying me. Despite my attempt to be nonchalant, I knew my behavior wasn't going unnoticed. At least by her. James seemed merely disappointed.

"Well, Formann's *is* pretty nifty," Anna May drawled out. "We can't let her go it alone, Jimmy. If Blythe's is having a sale, Formann's is bound to be having one too."

James shrugged. "Sure. I suppose they'll have as good a selection as anywhere else. I'm game."

I quietly let out a breath as we turned toward Seventh.

J.W. Formann's Department Store was a tan art deco monolith. Wide red awnings shaded the windows where merchandise was displayed. The interior of the first floor was a vast space of gray veined marble and glass display cases. Crystal chandeliers hung by the dozens from the high ceilings. I couldn't imagine coming in here alone, and I inwardly winced at how I'd so offhandedly told Anna May and James that I was going to pop inside for a look around.

James and I followed Anna May, passing case after case of merchandise until we were near the rear of the first floor. Anna May busied herself with a clerk who showed her pots of colored cream and powders. James and I hung back at another counter, which was full of jeweled headpieces and long necklaces. I took a sequined headband with a fluff of feathers and held it up to my forehead. "What do you think?"

"Very pretty." James picked up another hair accessory, a spray of paste diamonds, and pressed it against the side of his head.

I laughed, causing the clerk at the far end of the counter to spin around. Her brightly stained lips tightened and she twitched her head in a *no-no* rebuke.

James and I glanced at each other. Then our eyes skittered to the other counters, where customers were freely trying on jewelry and gloves.

Inwardly fuming, I fixed a wooden expression on my face, folded the headband, and laid it back with the others. James and I both stepped away from the counter. His neck was splotchy red all the way to his ears. The shy humor had fallen off his face. He slipped his hands into his pockets and stared at the floor until Anna May finished her transactions.

"We have to go to the fourth floor," Anna May said.

I wasn't sure if she had seen the clerk's disapproving gesture. Part of me wanted to suggest we leave, but I'd made such a fuss about coming here that I couldn't bring myself to make another one. And I sure didn't want to go back to Blythe's.

The cab was beginning to feel awfully tight. I hiked up a shoulder. "I'm of more use to them at home, and I actually like working in the store."

James blinked like I was making no sense. I studied my hands in my lap. He and Anna May were clearly waiting for a better answer. Part of me wanted to tell them to mind their own business, but of course that wouldn't help me make friends.

"I say, good for you!" Anna May broke the awkwardness. "I left school when I was sixteen."

"Yes, and what a blowout with Papa that caused." James pursed his lips and whistled.

Anna May shimmied her shoulders. "Well, I simply had bigger fish to fry."

"You mean the movies?" I prompted, desperate to take the attention off myself.

"Yep. Right after I made *Dinty*. Papa sure liked the money I made from that one, no matter what he thought of the role. And then I started to get bigger parts. There was *The First Born* and after that *Bits of Life* . . ." Her words drifted off and her gaze shifted to the front windshield. She seemed wistful, almost as if she did have regrets. "Once I got my first movie credit, I couldn't imagine sitting in a classroom."

James made a noise halfway between a sniff and a cough. It was almost rude, but Anna May jerked back to the present.

"I had to go at it full time, see if I could make a real go of it." The lightness was back in her voice. "You only need that high school degree if you're striking for college. I'm doing absolutely jake without it."

James rolled his eyes. "That's debatable."

"Don't roll your eyes at me, little brother. Who just bought you a one-hundred-dollar machine?"

My mouth dropped open at the price.

James inclined his head but retorted, "Once you buy me a coupe, then I'll admit you're doing quite fine."

Anna May reached across to pinch him. He tried to cower behind me. "Ruby, protect me!" he squealed in exaggerated high notes. I twisted around and landed a thick pinch on his arm through his suitcoat.

"Oh! Oh! So that's how it's going to be!" James raised and flexed a finger, if we do a bun in the back, tuck it under, and puff out the sides . . ."

Silently, I submitted to her primping, feeling peculiar and stiff. I imagined that white girls with waved hair and flaring knee skirts did this sort of thing with their mothers — getting ready for dates, talking about boys. But none of the Chinese girls I knew ever had. This newfound closeness made me uneasy. Not only was it unfamiliar, but it felt tainted, as if we intended to pull something over on James.

"There!" Ma declared with one last pat.

I angled my head left and right to see the sides of my hair in the tarnished mirror. Ma always wore her own hair in a low bun, and I'd half expected the hairdo to be matronly like hers. But with the bun tucked under, the waves, and a side part, the style resembled a marcelled bob. It flattered me, making my neck seem especially long.

"It's nice, Ma," I said. "I should go. I'm going to meet him at the movie house." I collected my handbag from a hook beside the stairs and started down.

"Ruby!" Ma's tone turned grave. I paused on the step.

"You heard what your ba said. He was serious, and you must take this boy seriously."

"I'm not going to trick him into wanting to marry me," I snapped. "I'm not getting married!"

"Phsh! This doesn't have to be a trick. It isn't! If you like him and he likes you, that's enough. Nothing has to happen right away. It would be enough to have an arrangement in place. A boy — well, a Chinese boy — doesn't allow himself to be seen with a girl unless he has real intentions."

I didn't think that was true anymore. At least not of James Wong. Like me, he seemed more American than traditional Chinese. "Don't get your hopes up, Ma."

Ma rubbed her neck. "I hope this isn't a mistake to let you go with him. It's a big risk to be seen with a boy. You have to be . . . modest." She bit her lip and shifted her eyes away from me. I knew she was alluding to Russell. The closest she would come to speaking about it, enough to remind me of what had gotten me into this mess. "Just try to be . . . Try to be a bit more . . . soft. It won't hurt you not to talk so much. Until you know what sort of person he is."

It was nuts that she was giving me advice about boys. What did she know about boys? Especially boys born in America.

"Sometimes you must hold back a little. You're too strong-willed. You show that part too soon and a boy won't know how to handle it." She crossed over and put her hand on mine, which was gripping the post. "Boys don't like girls who are too free."

I pulled my hand away.

"I have to go," I said and beat it down the stairs.

James was waiting in front of the California Theatre on Main Street, a few blocks from Chinatown. His hands were jammed in his pockets, and he craned his neck over the passersby, watching for me with an eager, anxious expression. The look made me smile to myself. It was enough to erase all of Ma's irritating advice. When he spotted me, his face lit up, and I dashed across the street.

"Hi!" James grinned down at me. "We have to hurry."

"Sure. Sorry for running late."

We rushed up to the box office and he paid for our ten-cent seats. We crossed the lobby and entered the darkened theater. The movie and the music — a heavy, moody score — had already started.

James moved past the back rows, which were crowded with couples. I followed him to the middle of the room, and we dropped into seats. The film was an English historical drama, *Beau Brummel.* I started to whisper a comment about the big dresses and all the puffy wigs, but his attention was already locked on the picture.

An intertitle appeared on the screen: *You know how they forced me to give you up!*

Russell guttered into mind and my face grew hot. I was glad it was dark, although James was too engrossed in the picture to notice anyway.

The story turned out to be about a British military officer, George "Beau" Brummel, whose true love, Margery, was pressured into marrying someone else. It was hardly what was happening to me, but

the story still dug a little too close to the bone. When the two lovers were caught in an embrace by Margery's mother — *Would you ruin us for this nobody?* — I went rigid.

*Revenge was all he thought of now . . .*

My ears burned. I tried to push Russell out of my mind, but my thoughts slid about, half focused on the demoralizing drama as George fell into poverty, half drifting to my own predicament.

*Four months. By the time I return . . .*

It was still hard to believe Ba was serious. He couldn't drag me onto a ship and force me to marry someone on the other side of the world.

Could he?

I would run away first.

The film plodded on. The white light from the screen gleamed on James's face, his lips parted in a faint frown. I turned back to the flicker, charmed and a little surprised to see him so touched by George's sad situation.

James was sweet. I knew he liked me, but Ma's idea that we were going to come to some arrangement in such a short time was too ridiculous.

Still, maybe if Ba saw that something was developing between us . . .

The movie ended with George, overwhelmed by despair, calling up Margery's ghostly image until he fell over dead himself. I had to stifle a scoff. The lights came on in the theater. We shuffled outside with the rest of the crowd, blinking as our eyes adjusted to the searing afternoon sun.

"Wasn't that great?" James said. Moviegoers streamed past us and clotted the sidewalk, studying the posters encased in glass.

I searched for a diplomatic response. "It was a bit on the long side, but I liked the costumes. The budget must've been huge."

"Long! It didn't feel long to me."

"You seemed so drawn into the story." I gave him a teasing smile.

"I guess I didn't realize it was going to be a romance, but you liked it, right?" He sounded so earnest, I couldn't tell him I'd found the picture depressing and melodramatic.

Instead I said, "Did you see how they made Margery and George appear as ghosts at the end? I've never seen that effect before. I wonder how they did it."

"I'll have to ask Anna May if she knows." James shuffled his feet and gazed down the street as if he didn't know what to do next. "Well, I guess we should head home."

Saturday afternoon meant throngs of people on the sidewalk — young and old couples, women in pastel dresses clutching kids and handbags, everyone moving at a leisurely pace. The late-day sun had softened the air.

I found myself doing most of the talking as we ambled toward Chinatown. James, with his hands in his pockets, seemed much more reserved than the day we'd purchased his typewriter. In no hurry to be home, I walked slowly and chattered about San Francisco — until my eye landed on a two-story house.

"Why did you move?" he asked.

"What was that?" I was distracted by a sign nailed to a porch post: *Rooms to Rent*.

"Why did your family move from San Francisco?"

I was still stuck on that sign, but I tore my attention away and told James about

Ba, the emporiums he'd worked for, the money he'd saved.

By then we had come to the Chinese Opera House, an outdoor stage facing a courtyard full of benches. The actors, with their brightly painted faces and their satiny red and gold gowns, wailed out songs. There was a good crowd today — mostly men, but a small group of women sat in a corner at the back, splitting melon seeds between their teeth. Much of the audience chatted, only half-listening to the show. A few kids chased one another with sticks and clacked on roller skates at the rear of the pavilion.

"Do you want to watch?" James asked.

I eyed the crowd. If James and I sat down together, we'd be noticed. Curious glances would turn to scrutiny. I couldn't afford to be the topic of neighborhood tittle-tattle. "I'd better get home and help my ma with supper."

James nodded. "I'll walk with you."

We headed to the alley at the back of the shop, keeping a respectable distance between us. Compared to the street, the alley was dim and cool. Deserted. James made no move to close the space between us, but that intoxicating stirring came over me. He liked me. I sensed that he wanted to kiss me. I slowed, hoping he would stop us before we reached my back door. The attraction was there for me too, a slow, steady thrum.

With Russell, the feeling had been like a buzz that wouldn't —

I sharply turned my face away from James, suddenly aware, confused, that Russell had crept into my head again.

I heaved him out with a quiet exhale, then stopped several yards away from my door.

"This is me." I flipped my hand vaguely.

James nodded. His gaze flicked to the door, along the alley, then to the ground. I wondered how many girlfriends he'd had. He was so nice-looking, I couldn't imagine that he was shy with girls, yet I could sense his awkwardness. I wanted to reach out and pull him toward me, but despite my annoyance with her advice, what Ma had said about being modest needled me.

I went to the door and put my hand on the knob. "I suppose I'll see you."

"Ruby." James pressed a hand against the door to prevent me from opening it. I turned my face up to him. His gaze was on my mouth, full of longing. But he didn't move. The moment stretched long. Too long.

I glanced down the alley. There was no one in sight. *Hang it all*, I thought.

I stood up on my toes and kissed him.

Ma was wringing out underclothes at the sink when I came in. She twisted around as I pulled the door shut, her mouth parted, ready with questions.

"It was fine, Ma," I said before she could ask. My lips were swollen from the kiss, and I moved toward the stairs to avoid questions, but Ma wasn't having it.

"Good, good! Now wait!" She gave the cloth another good squeeze, shook it out, and gestured at me to hang it up.

I set my handbag on a stack of crates. Ma moved aside so I could reach the drying rack above the sink, which she had lowered on its pulley.

She watched me as I pinned up the clothes. I knew she wanted to hear more

But first I had to get work. And telling Ma that I was going to the movies with James was my cover. If I got hired on somewhere, I supposed I'd have to tell her, but no need to get her all riled up before anything was settled.

# 11

In the small waiting area outside the employment office of J.W. Formann's Department Store, a secretary with gray-streaked hair guarded a suite of offices. She looked up as I approached her desk.

What was I doing here? My knees felt weak, and for a second I considered spinning on my heel and trotting back to the elevator.

"May I help you?" she asked.

I straightened my spine and smoothed my blue cotton frock. "I wondered if there are any open positions for counter girls." I hoped my voice didn't betray my nervousness. "I'd like to apply."

She rose and rapped on the office door. A brass nameplate etched with the words *Personnel Director* was nailed in the center.

"Come in!" a deep voice called out.

She poked her head inside. "Mr. Haber, there's a girl here who wants to apply for a place on the counters."

"Oh, good! Send her in!"

She pushed the door open for me. The office was paneled in dark wood and had a row of oak filing cabinets against one wall. The room had a cavernous feeling despite the windows behind the desk — which was well-ordered with a blotter, a lamp, a telephone, and a wire basket of papers weighed down by a pair of scissors. Mr. Haber set down a letter opener and pushed his chair back a few inches. He had taken off his suit coat, and his middle-aged paunch strained against his vest.

"Your name?"

"Ruby Chan, sir."

He pursed his lips under a neatly clipped moustache, which had been oiled with pomade to hold its center part, same as his hair. I knew it was his job to size up potential employees, but I didn't like the way his eyes traveled the length of my body, much like the way Auntie Matchmaker had inspected me. I tried not to fidget.

"You're seeking a counter position? Have you any experience in sales?"

"Yes, sir. My father owns a store. I help there with displays, bookkeeping, and customers."

"A store? What type of store?" He picked up a pen and began to roll it between his fingers, his arm outstretched with his wrist resting on the edge of the desk.

"Decorative goods, antiques, and furniture."

"Oh yes? Where is this store? And whyever are you seeking employment elsewhere?"

"It's in Chinatown, sir. Chan's Art Emporium." I hadn't anticipated his last question, and I fumbled for an answer. "I thought . . . I thought it would be . . . a new experience to work in a large department store such as this."

"Hmm." His moustache rode up and down like a wooly worm as he twiddled his lips, studying me.

Although I arranged my face in a polite mask, I felt I hadn't given the right answer. Maybe I should've taken a different tone. Shown more eagerness. Or desperation?

"I can offer you a spot on the elevators. Nine to six Tuesday through Friday, and eight to one on Saturdays. We close early on Saturday because Mr. Formann believes the staff should enjoy the weekend afternoon off."

"Elevators?" The question slipped out before I could think.

"Yes."

I'd overheard him say, *Oh, good!* when his secretary told him someone was looking for a place on counters. So why wasn't he posting me there? Was I being slighted because I was Chinese?

"Is there nothing at counters then?" I ventured, keeping my expression impassive.

"I don't have anything for you in counters. Elevators is where I need you. The pay is ten dollars a week."

*For you.*

I could apply somewhere else. There were dozens of other department stores in the city. Anna May had worked at Ville de Paris. How had she gotten hired on? I imagined she'd sailed in and everyone had fallen over themselves to give her that place. But I was no Anna May, and time was short with no guarantee that I'd find anything better. "That will be fine," I said.

"Good!" Mr. Haber leaned forward and pulled a drawer open and began to rifle through it. "Now, do you have any Chinese dresses?"

I canted my head, uncertain that I'd heard him correctly.

"A Chinese dress," Mr. Haber repeated impatiently. "Do you have one?"

There was the cheongsam I wore for Chinese celebrations. I nodded.

"Excellent! We like our elevator girls to have a little flair if it's possible. It gives the store a bit more *atmosphere*." He pulled out a card and pushed it across his desk. "Fill this out. You can start tomorrow."

My eyes narrowed. He was taking me on because I was Chinese, a novelty, an ornament. The slight was too familiar, but it was also why I needed the job.

I bent down and signed the slip.

picturing me being eaten up by the White Devil. "You can't. It's not . . ." She sputtered, at a loss for words.

I knew she didn't mind the idea of my working so much. Ma used to do piecework herself, but the materials had always been delivered to our home. What bothered her was the working in public, in the general public outside of Chinatown. Good Chinese girls didn't put themselves in front of people. If I were working with other girls shelling shrimp in a warehouse, or sewing garments in a factory, or even helping a lady customer in our store, that would be one thing, but *out there* was another story.

I turned away, checking my purse for streetcar fare and a handkerchief. "Ma, it's a nice department store. Very upscale. It's where Anna May and James bought his typewriter. I'll be working in the ladies' department." A white lie; it would be easier on her if she thought I'd be interacting mostly with women. That was much more respectable than being an elevator girl.

"Wait a minute!" Ma's stool scraped the floorboards. "Your ba would never allow —"

"Oh, Ma!" I snapped my purse shut and spun around. "Ba's not here now! I can't sit around the house all day. If I can't work in the shop, I have to do something besides dusting and" — I flipped my hand at the sink, to the stove, and then up the stairs toward our rooms — "all this home stuff!"

Her mouth pinched. I could see how hurt and angry she was. I had insulted her whole life.

"I'll quit before he gets back from the trip." I softened my tone. "He won't have to know. And the money — I need it for clothes and things if I'm going to . . . go out . . ." I allowed my words to trail off. Let her think that I wanted to dress up for dates with James. It was oily of me, but I had no choice. "I have to go! I can't be late on my first day."

I turned to the alley door, holding my breath, hoping she wasn't going to stop me. I was taking advantage of catching her off guard, but I didn't know what else to do.

"Don't worry, Ma! I'll be back by dinner."

Out on the street, a couple of shopkeepers sweeping the walks in front of their stores gave me double takes as I went by. I supposed seeing a girl my age wearing a cheongsam on a Tuesday morning was cause to raise an eyebrow, even in our neighborhood. But once I was out of Chinatown, the cheongsam really began to draw attention, despite its muted pattern. Steeling myself against the creep of self-consciousness, I walked briskly to the trolley stop. A couple of glances from passersby were unmistakably hostile, but gradually I registered that others were merely curious, maybe even admiring. I kept my head up and eyes forward.

I reported to Mr. Haber's office with five minutes to spare, but his secretary led me to another door and tapped on it before pushing it open.

"Excuse me, Miss Buckner, I have the new elevator girl here."

Miss Buckner, tall and reedy, stood at the side of her desk, flicking through some papers. Her sashed suit hung on her thin shoulders as if it were on a hanger. She peered at me over her reading glasses, her eyes taking in my cheongsam, making me conscious of how it strained against my bust.

"Thank you, Miss Lester. I'll take it from here," she said.

Miss Lester left, and Miss Buckner took off her glasses. "Did Mr. Haber ask you to wear that dress?"

"Yes, ma'am."

Her eyelids fluttered almost imperceptibly. "All right." She moved toward the door. "Follow me."

I trailed after her down the hall to two elevators, where she pushed the button.

"These are the staff elevators. All employees are required to use these elevators unless they are escorting customers." The doors opened and she pushed aside the interior metal grate, then closed it after we stepped in. "All our elevators have been modernized with automatic leveling and push buttons, so all you will have to do is manage the interior grate and push the button for the floor. The outside doors will close automatically."

Miss Buckner pressed the button marked B. The elevator descended with a loud hum, clicking at each passing floor. When we arrived at the basement level, she didn't move. I didn't understand why she just stood there with her hands clasped until she glanced at me and ticked her head toward the door. I hurried to pull open the grate.

In the women's room, she assigned me a locker, then showed me how to clock in and out. After that I followed her to the main elevator bank.

"You've been assigned Elevator Number Six. You're also in charge of keeping the cab neat and tidy. One of the other operators can show you where the brooms and mops are kept if you require them." She briskly explained how to manage a crowd of customers getting on and off various floors and going in different directions. The early mornings were busy with bargain shoppers, and then the regular shoppers would begin to arrive around ten o'clock, she reported.

"I will now take you on a tour of the store. You are responsible for knowing the location of every department so that you can direct customers as needed."

We stepped into the cab, which was paneled with an art deco pattern of inlaid wood and had brass railings on three sides. I drew the gate across and pushed all the buttons just as Miss Buckner instructed. We disembarked at each floor but went no farther than the elevator lobby. Miss Buckner gestured toward each department as she reeled off the names. That was the tour.

"Excuse me, Miss Buckner," I said as we arrived back on the fifth floor, "is there a listing of the departments I can use to help me remember their locations?"

"There's a directory on each floor. You may ask one of the other operators to show you where it is. Now, if you find yourself in a lull, you are to descend to the main level and station yourself just outside the door. If you are in view of the customers, you must stand with upright posture, evenly balanced on both legs. You will get tired, but there is to be no slumping or leaning against a wall in the presence of our patrons. Remember, you are on duty. You are not here to socialize with the staff or to chitchat with the other operators or customers. Here at Formann's we adhere to a strict code of propriety." Her eyelids fluttered again.

I nodded.

"We will be observing you to ensure that you maintain the standard." She glanced once more at my cheongsam before she left me. I wished I had a standard uniform.

The morning was busy. I started to learn the ropes and ducked out every chance I got to study the directory map. A couple of times I glimpsed the other operators on the main floor, stiffly positioned outside their cabs, waiting for customers. They were all men and they all wore the uniform.

At my lunch break, I bought a ham salad sandwich in the employee canteen and ate alone at a table in the corner, pretending to take no notice of the counter girls and salesclerks talking and eating in mixed company. Most of them were in their twenties, it seemed to me — maybe in their late teens, but certainly older than I was. There were a few looks thrown my way, not especially friendly, so I kept my expression bland as I chewed, the bread tasteless in my mouth.

Somehow I made it through the day, and at six o'clock I went down to the women's room and gathered my handbag. The room was in a frenzy of girls removing their store smocks and fluffing their hair and putting on hats.

I squeezed through to my locker. The laughter and chatter diminished as the other girls noticed me. At the next locker over, a girl with frizzy brown curls applied lipstick behind a small gold compact. The tube stalled on her mouth as she caught sight of me. I gave her a tentative smile. She nodded back without smiling. Her eyes skittered down to my cheongsam, and I braced myself for some rude look or remark.

Instead, her face brightened. "That's the nobbiest little dress," she said.

Her cheery tone was a welcome surprise. "Thanks, I like yours too." I gestured at her pleated pink frock.

"I've seen those dresses in the pictures," she said, "but they're usually plastered in flowers. Where'd you get that one?"

"My mother made it. I picked out the fabric. It's called a cheongsam." Ma had wanted me to choose a traditional pattern, but I'd insisted on the simple design.

A few girls around us had quieted, openly listening to our conversation.

"You're working here?" she asked.

"Yes. I'm on elevators."

"Elevators? Why aren't you in uniform?"

"I'm not sure. I was told to wear a Chinese dress."

Another girl, fixing on a bucket hat, chimed in. "I'll tell you why." She flashed her eyebrows up and down like Charlie Chaplin. "She's a touch of the exotic at the all-American Formann's Department Store."

The other girls tittered. Heat crept up the back of my neck.

"Don't pay any attention to her." The girl with the frizzy curls licked her finger and slid it across a few strands on her forehead to flatten them down. "We're all expected to be bright things, easy on the eyes." She snapped the compact closed and slipped it into the clutch tucked under her arm. "But that means you gotta mind your backside."

# 13
## JUNE 1924

On the Thursday afternoon of my third week at Formann's, a dapper fella in a raglan suit strode onto the elevator.

"What floor, sir?" I asked.

"Well, hello there." A smile turned up the corners of his lips as he planted himself in the center of the cab.

I pulled the gate closed and repeated, "What floor?"

I'd come to understand what the girl in the locker room had meant when she said *a touch of the exotic*, what Mr. Haber had meant by *atmosphere*. Young children stared at me. Older women in rayon dresses and thick stockings stuttered in their steps when they noticed me. The more stylish ladies with finger waves and cloche hats tilted their heads my way. The men never spoke to me if there were footsteps bore closer. Mr. Haber shook his head as if he'd forgotten what he was saying and then dismissed me with a wave.

I exited his office, feeling both annoyed and tense. As I was coming out, I saw it was Miss Buckner striding toward the offices. She paused, her eyes flitting over me for a moment, but she quickly recovered and charged past me.

"Mr. Haber, we have a problem with tomorrow's fashion show," I heard her say behind me.

I was in the elevator before I realized I was still clutching the bills in my fist. I sighed and stuffed them into my purse.

# 14

When I got off the Yellow Car near Chinatown, I hadn't taken five steps before I heard my name called amid the clamor of rush hour.

I whirled around to see James on the last step of the trolley's doors. He waved, hopped off, and skirted around the folks waiting to get on. His typewriter case bumped against his leg.

"We were on the same car!" I laughed. "I didn't even see you!"

"I guess I didn't see you either. Not until I was getting off." He caught sight of my cheongsam and a puzzled look came over his face. "Where are you coming from?"

"My new place of employment, Formann's. You're looking at their newest elevator operator."

magazine until I came to the four-page spread about the movie. *Here is magic! Here is beauty! Here is the answer to the cynics who give the motion picture no place in the family arts . . . It is a work of rare genius . . .*

Douglas Fairbanks was featured in the interview, but there were also several overlapping images of the flicker — including one of Anna May scantily clad as a Mongol slave.

I had seen that exact image before, weeks back when I skipped classes one afternoon to go for a drive with Russell.

I'd met up with him a block away from school. The Ford's motor was already running when I slipped into the passenger side. We roared off, first heading west through what Russell called Mortuary Row because so many funeral businesses had set up shop there, then going north on Westlake Avenue toward Hollywood.

I was giddy, riding in a motorcar, windows rolled down. With a boy. The streets were wide open, lined with telephone poles — their wires crisscrossing overhead — and narrow sidewalks sprouting fiddleneck weeds and yellow mustard. Dust swirled as we sped past pepper trees and Mexican palms.

"Ever been out this way?"

I hadn't. We'd been in Los Angeles for just a couple of months, and the only times I'd ventured out of Chinatown were for school and piano.

"My pop says Los Angeles is growing like crazy. Hey, look, there goes the Hollywood Red Car."

He pointed at a bright red trolley with orange trim detail, so shiny that it looked like it'd just been painted. It coasted along its track in the same direction we were headed.

"The Red Cars go out all around Southern California — you can jump on one and swing out to Long Beach or Santa Monica or the Valley. It's all movie studios here, though."

Russell stuck his arm out the window, leaving it outstretched as we motored past huge lots — some gated and stately, others cluttered with buildings that appeared to have been thrown together in a hurry.

"The flicker biz is why people are pouring into the city. Did you know you can given me yesterday lurched into my head. I had been holding them when I'd come out of his office, and all at once I realized what Miss Buckner was thinking. What she thought she'd seen. Heat crept up the back of my neck. I opened my mouth to tell her I didn't want to be in the show, but she whipped her finger up to hush me.

"Mr. Haber is adamant about this. Now you run up to Alterations on the sixth floor. Miss Lacey, the Ready-to-Wear manager, will meet you there. Once you're fitted, you will return to your post at the elevators until a half hour before the show, which begins at noon. Miss Lacey and Miss Adams, the Displays manager, will instruct you in the protocol." She tucked her chin back. "I assure you, it will be just this one time."

When I passed through the double doors of Alterations, I was greeted by the loud rattling of electric sewing machines. Three women hunched over the machines at a worktable in the back of the room, where a wall of tall windows flooded the space with light. To my left, a row of curtained dressing rooms lined one wall. The rest of the room was filled with clothing racks, fitting platforms, and more tables. Every accessory I could imagine — scarves, purses, hats, parasols — sat waiting to be matched with the right outfit. For a moment I just stood there, taking it all in: the flashes of color, the blur of activity.

"Are you the lucky girl today?" A woman in a celery-green linen suit popped out from behind a long rack of dresses.

"I'm Ruby. Miss Buckner sent me."

"I'm Miss Lacey." She was easily my mother's age, but she wore her chestnut hair styled in a sleek cut, and dangly earrings brushed her shoulders. "Well, well, well. Come on over here."

I joined her in front of a three-sided mirror in the corner beside the dressing rooms.

"Wherever did they dig you up?" Miss Lacey's red painted lips curved up in a wide smile as she inspected me. I suppressed my flash of annoyance at being looked over like a shop window dummy. She twirled her finger, gesturing that I should turn around.

"I'm an elevator girl."

the staff elevator. On the seventh floor she passed us over to Miss Adams, who managed the show. She took us to a corridor that connected the kitchen to the rooftop restaurant.

"So, you're our replacement girl today?" Miss Adams sported a pleated skirt and a tucked white blouse with a loose tie around her neck. "Pulled from the floor?"

I nodded.

"Okay, I'll cue you when to start. Miss Lacey will be announcing what each girl is wearing. When it's your turn, you'll step up onto that platform between those two big planters over there. You'll see how Meg moves before you go on. Do what she does, but don't get jumpy and rush. Set your pace to hers. We can't have everyone clumping up. Once you go through the pavilion you'll pass through the other doors and that's when you run down the stairs and change as quick as you can. The elevator will be waiting to bring you back up here. You've got to be quick because with just eight models your next walk will come up fast."

I nodded numbly at the deluge of instructions, latching on to *do what she does*.

Miss Adams went to the head of the line. The music stopped as Miss Lacey stepped onto the platform to introduce the show. When the ensemble resumed with a light jazzy tune, Miss Adams began to turn the girls out.

Before I knew it, I was next. I had a clear view of the restaurant space, which was shaded by a white wooden pergola threaded with fake greenery. Miss Adams nudged me, and somehow my feet unstuck themselves from the floor and I made it to the platform where Miss Lacey stood. A light breeze brushed my thighs, bringing up gooseflesh that I feared were as visible as hives. The pergola offered little shade. I could feel the sun on my shoulders, and the brightness dazzled me, but I kept my face upturned, focusing on the fronds of the potted palms as I tried to block out all the ladies at the tables.

"Now, Ruby, if you'll just turn around." Miss Lacey twirled a finger.

I rotated as she finished reading the card that described the suit, then moved onto the floor when she gestured for me to step down.

I scanned the pavilion for Meg. Instead I saw Mr. Haber standing off to the side. I pivoted away, only to see two ladies with their heads together whispering as they pointed at me. The women at the other tables simpered as I wove past, or so I imagined. I tried not to rush as I trailed Meg, pausing and dipping a knee or putting a hand on my hip in a half-hearted imitation of her. I told myself I was no more than a moving plaster mannequin. That got me through, and soon the exit at the other end of the pavilion was mercifully in sight.

I nearly tripped when Anna May Wong appeared in front of me.

She was wearing a wide modish hat of tightly woven straw that was vaguely shaped like a Chinese farmer's hat. She stepped aside as one of the models sailed past her, then paused to take in the show. Her eyes landed on me, and she grinned and cocked her head in an exaggerated show of approval.

Another wave of self-consciousness ran through me, but I also wanted to laugh. I flashed her a smile as she slipped into a seat at a vacant table at the back of the pavilion.

Anna May was probably no stranger to department store fashion parades, but I was surprised to see her here today of all days. There was no time to dwell on it as I exited the restaurant area and dashed downstairs to change.

By the time I took my second promenade, the women seated around Anna May were craning their necks her way. Anna May kept her attention on the models, with a pleasant expression on her face. She seemed unaware of the flutter she was causing. Or she was very good at ignoring it.

I pulled my own shoulders back and twirled my parasol as Ms. Lacey concluded the show to light applause from the diners. I went through the exit and dashed toward the stairwell in the corridor.

"Ruby, wait!"

I turned. Anna May hurried over.

"What a surprise to see you in the show!" she said. "All in the flesh."

I winced and lowered the parasol so it covered my thighs. "I know. They pulled me from my post as a last-minute replacement. What are you doing here?"

"I was heading out to buy some accessories to go with the dress I plan to wear in a flicker. James mentioned you were working here so I decided to wiggle on over. When I asked for you at the elevator, the operator said you'd been sent up to do this gig. Naturally, I had to see for myself. No need to look so mortified! You were just great! Will this be a regular post for you?"

I grimaced. "I don't think so. I hope not, anyway."

"It's got to be better than elevators, right? But I thought you were keen to work at your family's shop."

When I gave her the line about the store not doing well, she clicked her tongue and said, "Gosh darn, I should've thought of your shop for the frilly bits to complement my outfit. Do you think you have anything to suit?"

"Oh, yes! I could really show you some nice things! Could you swing by there tomorrow afternoon? I only work half days here on Saturdays." My mind skittered around, cataloguing the accessories we had at the shop. Then, over Anna May's shoulder, I saw Mr. Haber enter the corridor from the pavilion.

"Please come," I said to Anna May. "But now I'd better get go —"

"Ruby?" Mr. Haber spotted me. "What are you still —"

Anna May turned when she heard my name called.

Mr. Haber's face lit up. "Hello! Is this who I think it is?" He hurried over, his moustache stretching wide over his lip.

"Yes, Mr. Haber," I said. "May I present Miss Anna May Wong?"

"Hello, Miss Wong!" He bowed a little, then rocked back on his heels. "What an honor to meet you." There were practically stars in his eyes. His glance shifted between Anna May and me, and I could feel his regard for me rising.

"You came to see Ruby in the show?" He looked almost giddy. Did he think I'd asked her to come — left my post and rushed to ring up my movie-star friend so she could watch me march around in bathing suits? "She did quite well, don't you think?" He was preening, apparently forgetting that he'd placed me in the show just this morning.

Anna May inclined her head. "She did."

"And you! I've been reading about you, the splash you're making in *The Thief of Bagdad*. The wife and I are quite excited to see it when it starts showing here in LA."

"That's very kind, Mr. Haber."

"And it was very kind of you to attend our show. Do you do any modeling yourself?"

"Well, not in a few years. I've not had the time."

"Yes, yes, I understand. These fashion teas and luncheons are nothing compared to the pictures!"

"But they are fun." Anna May nudged me before turning back to Mr. Haber. "I don't know any woman who doesn't relish a good fashion parade."

"That's true!" Mr. Haber's head bounced eagerly. "Our shows are very popular. I wonder — would you consider modeling for us in a show sometime?"

"Oh." The question obviously caught Anna May off guard. "I don't know —"

"It would be such a boon to the store," Mr. Haber said. "You could walk alongside Ruby here."

I wasn't going to do any more modeling. I started to protest but Mr. Haber pressed on.

"We could make you the main feature of the show, Miss Wong." He spread his fingers out, then clasped his hands together. "My! What a treat it would be for our patrons!"

I knew he was right about that. Anna May knew how to carry herself, and with the new picture about to release here and all the press she'd been getting in the past few months, people were bound to be curious about her. Gooseflesh suddenly sprang up across my bare skin as an idea formed.

"Mr. Haber," I pushed in, "Anna May and I were just talking about Chinese dresses and the one she's going to wear in her next movie. If Formann's were to frame a show around her, what if the show had an Oriental theme?" I flitted my eyes to Anna May. "We could feature outfits made with Oriental textiles — embroidered jackets, patterned silks. I've seen several garments on the floor that could fit the theme with the right accessories."

Mr. Haber's moustache rode up and down. "We've had many themed shows, but I don't recall that we've had an Oriental one." His eyes shone at Anna May. She blinked as if a gnat was hovering too near her eye.

Of course, by "Oriental," Mr. Haber would understand me to mean looks and materials from any and all Eastern countries. But I was thinking in particular of showcasing Chinese fashions. After all, why shouldn't our styles be seen as equal to the latest trends from Europe, instead of mere curiosities? "We could call it . . . Shanghai Chic," I said. "Or something like that."

"Oh, that's clever," Anna May said.

"Would you do it, Miss Wong?" Mr. Haber took her hand and held it between his. Anna May stiffened but she didn't pull away.

"Miss Lacey and Miss Adams organize the shows for us, and they simply do wonders with the themes," he went on. "I'm sure they would put together the most elegant affair if you agreed to be part of it."

Anna May graciously squeezed Mr. Haber's hand before she drew hers out of his clamshell clasp. I could see her turning the proposition over in her mind. She studied me with a reserved expression, doubtless wondering why I'd suggested the theme after making faces about modeling.

If Mr. Haber hadn't been standing there, I would've told her: No, I didn't want to push an elevator button for the rest of the summer — or for the foreseeable future if I had to leave home. I didn't care about modeling, but the Displays Department was interesting, and I could see myself working with Miss Lacey and Miss Adams. A project like this might help me get my foot in with them.

"It would be awfully nice to showcase the culture . . ." Anna May said, trailing her words.

I held my breath. She just had to say yes.

"Mr. Haber, did you know Ruby's family has a store in Chinatown that specializes in art and furniture?" Anna May turned to me. "Wouldn't it be fitting if your family's store supplied some decorative touches for the show? Wall hangings, screens, lanterns and such?"

I blinked, surprised by the suggestion, but nodded along.

"For a fee, of course," Anna May added, addressing Mr. Haber again. "In the pictures, the sets are often outfitted with fine pieces rented from shops like Chan's. You could certainly elevate your production by doing the same."

My heart leaped. It was a fantastic idea. She was a doll to suggest it.

"Yes, yes, perhaps I can talk to Miss Adams about that." Mr. Haber looked like he would promise her anything.

I threw Anna May another hopeful look. She still hadn't agreed to headline the show.

"Well, then," she said, "I suppose this Shanghai chick will be appearing in Shanghai Chic at J.W. Formann's Department Store."

# 16

Anna May showed up at the shop on Saturday near closing time. As soon as I heard her voice, I rushed out from the back room where I'd been going over the ledger. There she stood with a dress box under her arm. She was wearing the white middy blouse I'd seen her in the first time we met. When she spotted me, she turned away from Mr. Lew and said, "Ruby, there you are! I'm ready for you to show me all the pretty things!"

I threw Mr. Lew a silent plea to let me do it. So far, he'd respected Ba's wishes, keeping me to the books during business hours and letting me clean only after the store was closed. But when I had told him about Shanghai Chic — leaving out the part about modeling — he'd been pleased with the scheme to rent pieces to Formann's.

Mr. Lew rose from the chair behind Ba's little desk. "I'll check over the books." He went to the back, leaving me with Anna May.

"It's so good to see you!" I told her. "I wanted to thank you for agreeing to do the show and for suggesting they use our pieces. That was such a clever idea! Mr. Lew and I went through the shop last night selecting things we thought would work for the rooftop pavilion."

She waved off my thanks. "Well, the theme was a pretty sharp idea itself. I'm always game to show off all things Chinese and shine a spotlight on the culture."

"And you're the perfect person to do it," I said eagerly. "To show the world the best things about our culture."

"I don't know about that," she said with a little laugh. "But it'll be interesting to see what they come up with."

A lot did hinge on Miss Lacey and Miss Adams, I thought. They'd be the ones choosing the outfits and the décor. Shanghai Chic would reflect *their* ideas of China — of the East in general — as much as anything else, but I didn't see a way around that.

I gestured to the box. "Is that the dress for the movie?"

"Yes." She opened the box and pulled out a slender gray velvet dress with thin shoulder straps and a curlicue pattern of beading down one side. "It's not a particularly Oriental style, which is what they'll really want, but I thought I'd try something a little different. That's why I need an accessory or two to give it that Eastern flair."

"What's the part?" I asked.

Anna May scoffed lightly. "A manipulative vamp of some vague Eastern heritage."

I wrinkled my nose. "You make being a movie star sound awfully unglamorous."

She chuckled and shrugged. "It does get a little tiring doing the same ol' thing."

I knew she meant the submissive or conniving female roles that so many in the Chinese community judged her for. The roles that embarrassed her family. "I can imagine. Have you tried for different parts?"

"Ha! There aren't any other parts for us. At least not yet. I'm not allowed to play a proper leading lady because apparently audiences won't tolerate me kissing a white person. Among other reasons. Of course, they don't want to give any leading roles to us. Even if the lead characters are Oriental, most of the time they're played by white actors." She blinked irritably and then shook her head as if to fling off her annoyance. "But you know what, Ruby" — her face suddenly brightened — "I've got my own production company in the works! And I'm going to make films about *us*."

"You mean the Chinese? Chinatown?"

"Yes. All different stories about us based on our culture, history, ancient myths, everything. And other Eastern cultures as well. None of that Oriental villain garbage, lumping us all together."

"You can do that? Just up and start your own company and make whatever movies you want?"

Anna May shimmied her shoulders. "Well, that's what this town is all about, isn't it? Since *The Thief*, people have begun to take interest in me. I thought, why shouldn't I do what other actors have done and set up my own shop? I'll find my own scenarioists to write the scripts, create the parts I want to play and give other Oriental actors some opportunities to shine. I have a partner who's helping me with the business end of it, raising the money we'll need to get started."

"That's wonderful!" My thoughts flickered back to the fashion show, and for a moment I imagined a whole host of Chinese American models wearing clothes chosen by Chinese American managers . . . and being watched by Chinese American customers too.

"I've got a lot to learn," said Anna May. "But in the meantime, I've got to keep the cameras on me until the financial backing starts rolling in." She held the dress up by the straps and flattened it against her body. "Even if it means playing the mantrap."

"Then let's find you the perfect accessory." I went to a case, slid the glass back, and pulled out a few headdresses — simple wedding crowns and some elaborate but smaller combs. "How about one of these? Something not too ornate, since the dress is fairly understated."

We spent the next twenty minutes holding various pieces against the dress, trying them on Anna May, and discussing how she'd style her hair. She eventually decided on a filagree headdress she would wear atop a turban — and a long strand of hand-carved carnelian beads, not necessarily for the costume.

"It'll be nice to wear something authentic, even if the role is not very original," Anna May said while I wrapped her purchases and made up her ticket. Once she'd paid, she moved toward a tall cabinet and traced the decorative carved wood of the door. "You have some lovely pieces here. I'm sure you're giving Fong See On a real run for his money."

"You think so? I wish our location was better, on Los Angeles Street or Marchessault, closer to the Plaza. There isn't as much foot traffic here. Since I've been home this summer, I've noticed the store isn't all that busy."

"I guess it takes time to build up the trade."

"Mr. Lew took Ba on to do just that. Hopefully when Ba gets all the new pieces, things will pick up. And with Formann's renting some of our things for the show, that's going to help keep us afloat."

Her gaze traveled around the store. "I may be needing some furniture soon."

"Really? Are you moving out on your own?"

"Sometimes I think about it." She sniffed. "I can't imagine living by myself, but sometimes my pop . . . ugh. He's in a snit about this new movie."

I thought of the photo of her in *Photoplay*. James's reaction. I imagined her ba's would've been even worse.

She shook her head as if she wanted to change the subject. "I'd better go. It's late and I was supposed to help Ma with dinner."

I handed her the package and followed her to the door. "I'm so glad you came!"

"Me too. I'll see you soon at the fashion parade. Or at the fitting. I suppose there'll be one ahead of the show."

She opened the door and paused, then nodded at someone standing just outside. When she sidestepped the newcomer, it took me a moment to register who it was.

As soon as Auntie Matchmaker saw me, she grinned and gestured to the back of

father will want to see all the options himself before he decides."

"Doesn't hurt to see which one the girl likes best. We can poke her ba toward the man you or the girl prefer. Makes it all go smoother." Auntie Matchmaker set down her bowl, dug an envelope out of her knitted reticule, and passed it to Ma.

Ma took the envelope and slid out a folded piece of paper. She shot me a cautioning look, as if she sensed my urge to snatch it and tear it to shreds. She laid it on the table beside her bowl, unopened, but I feared she was curious about the matches.

Auntie Matchmaker gestured to the paper with her chopsticks. "Now, the two best candidates are Fook Ping Shui and Chung Suey Wo, both well-established businessmen. One owns a very large dry goods store in Butte. That's in Montana . . ."

Montana!

"And the other has a smaller grocery store in San Francisco."

Maybe that should've sounded more appealing — after all, San Francisco still felt like home — but my mind could only grasp that both these men were strangers.

Ma threw me another glance. She set down the envelope, and got up to fill the kettle.

"It took them some years for their businesses to take hold," Auntie Matchmaker continued between bites, "so they're both in their mid-thirties. There're a few others on the list — older ones who are richer, younger ones who aren't so well set yet. You study them, but the two at the top of the list are the best. There are photographs in there as well."

Mr. Lew rose from the table. "I'd better close up the shop," he said to Ma. He nodded at Auntie Matchmaker, then said to me, "And you'd better come in and choose your husband."

Auntie Matchmaker, following Ma's eyes, twisted around. "Oh, you're still there! Come in, come in."

Reluctantly, I took two steps forward as Mr. Lew passed back into the store.

"Is Sissy getting married?" Danny asked. Ma shushed him.

"Did you hear who I found for you?" Auntie Matchmaker asked. "Even though so many of the men worry that American-born girls won't make good wives, they don't have much choice since entry into the country is tightening again for us. Very difficult for girls from China to come in now. And if the men go back home to find a wife, they may have trouble getting back in. You're lucky to have so many options."

I couldn't even muster a polite response.

Joe picked up the envelope and examine the photograph prints inside. Auntie Matchmaker took them out of his hand and passed them back to Ma before she continued to address me.

"But I assured these men that you will be a proper wife. Last time I was here your father said you were doing some Shu needlework. Have you finished it yet? Bring it down so I can see it, eh?"

For a second, I didn't know how to respond. Ba had let her think Ma's coverlet was mine, but the pillow covering *I* had been working on was a mess of tangled strings. I hadn't even picked it up since Ba left. A few days ago the boys had accidentally kicked over the big basket I'd been storing it in, and the piece had been trampled as they chased each other around.

"But it's still not finished yet." Ma rattled the cups. "Such a complicated piece." I knew she was feeling guilty for having to keep up Ba's lie. I would've laughed if I weren't so steamed up. The complete nonsense of his framing me as an ideal wife, and of Ma carrying on with the sham, was just too much.

I marched up the stairs. The drone of Auntie Matchmaker's voice floated after me as I pulled the clamp-frame out of the basket. The pillowcase had pulled free of the wooden pieces on one side. I carried it down and didn't even wait for Auntie Matchmaker to stop speaking to Ma before I thrust it at her.

Auntie Matchmaker pushed back her bowl, set the frame on the table, and straightened out the cloth. "What's this?" Bewildered, she squinted at me, then at Ma. At last she clicked her tongue and shook her head as she pushed the frame across the table.

I swept around to pick up the cup of tea that Ma had poured. "Yes, yes, take that to Mr. Lew," Ma said quickly as I marched out of the room.

they might not let him back in, why did he go?" It seemed reckless to have risked it.

"He's been planning this trip ever since he joined the business. Even with the new law looming, he was still determined to follow through. *More* determined. He wants to secure more business contacts so he doesn't have to go back and forth in the future. Your ba is stubborn like that, but clever too."

Auntie Matchmaker reentered the store, her cane striking the floorboards. "Your ma says that you haven't had a photograph taken yet." She blatantly eyed me up and down. Her inspection stopped at my breasts, and her lips pursed. "Such a pretty girl — a photograph can secure a better bride price for your family."

I bristled as she pulled my braid around and laid it on my chest.

"Put your hair in the front like this in the portrait. Undo the braids and leave it loose. A woman's hair is her greatest adornment, a way to present femininity without being immodest." She pointed at the door with her cane, gesturing for me to open it.

After she left, I turned back to Mr. Lew. "I don't understand Ba," I said. "I thought he was . . . different. Not so traditional. He's lived here for twenty-five years! How has he changed so little in all that time?"

Mr. Lew chuckled.

"What's so funny?"

"Your ba clings to the old ways because he has one foot back home. But he's very much of this country too. At home there's just the one culture, everyone's the same. He came here and sees the white people, the Mexicans, the Negroes, the American Indians, us. He sees what happens when all different people come to one place, how everyone is treated. He has a bigger picture of the world than you think. Keep that in mind."

*How everyone is treated.* I knew what he meant. The hostile and lewd looks, the insults, the laws. Everything meant to keep us in place.

"Well, *I'm* American," I spat out. "I was born here. I'm a born citizen!"

"You may be American on paper, but you have a Chinese face, and like your ba, you're Chinese to the bones."

We would see about that.

fit, but I'd asked Ma to nip in the waist and narrow the sleeves a tad. With the show in development — *my* show, I considered it — I didn't mind wearing the cheongsam to work anymore. Not if it was going to lead me to better things.

"It's called a cheongsam." I squared my shoulders back and dipped a knee, playing the model. "It's a traditional dress, but the socialites in Shanghai have modernized it by making it tight-fitting, with a slit up the side." I pointed to the exposed leg of a woman wearing a long cheongsam in an illustrated advertisement for Golden Valley Brandy. Of course, there was no slit in *my* dress.

"It's very alluring. I wonder if we couldn't come up with one or two of our own designs and get production started on them? Or take them on order." She seemed to be talking to herself as she continued to thumb through the periodicals. "These pictures are very helpful. They're giving me some ideas already."

I was thrilled. Not only because who knew what she might've come up on her own, but because she was open to my help.

"You're saving me quite a bit of work here," she added.

Which was just what I'd intended. "I'm so interested in merchandising and display. I've done some work in those areas at my family's art and antiques emporium. If there's anything else I can do to assist you or Miss Adams with the show, I'd love to be of service."

"Mr. Haber mentioned your family's store. I'm meeting with Miss Adams this afternoon and I can tell her that you've been in to see me."

"Will you let her know that we've already selected some pieces to show her, ones we think would work nicely in the pavilion?"

Miss. Lacey laughed. "Of course! She'll be as pleased with the assistance as I am."

That was what I was hoping for. I'd begun to imagine what would happen after the show. I pictured myself arranging a storefront window scene, maybe even coming up with the themes for the displays and helping to stage future fashion parades. I was determined to talk to Mr. Haber about moving into the Displays

Department after the show. But first I had to make sure everything went off perfectly.

The week was painfully long as I waited for Friday, when Miss Lacey had said I could drop by to see the outfits she'd pulled together for Shanghai Chic.

On Thursday evening, Mr. Lew told me that Miss Adams had come by the store that morning, approved most of the items we'd selected, and hadn't even blinked at the cost. I reveled in the news — and at the same time, I felt antsy to be directly involved with the show. Even if that meant sauntering around the restaurant with eyes all over me, I would do it. Being visible would remind everyone of how much I'd contributed, and if everything went well, my days of pushing buttons and pulling the elevator grate would soon be over.

When Friday finally arrived, I must've checked the clock at least twenty times before noon. I rushed up to Alterations and found Miss Lacey over by the dressing rooms. One of the models I recognized from the bathing suit show stood before a mirror, dressed in a gold-and-orange silk cocoon jacket with a vine-and-flower pattern. The cut of the jacket was clearly influenced by the Japanese kimono. My instinct was to point out to Miss Lacey that this didn't fit the theme of *Shanghai* Chic, but I checked myself. Of course, my vision of Chinese fashion was going to be lumped into a mishmash of Eastern styles. I would just have to make the best of it.

Miss Lacey examined the model in the mirror and frowned. "Maybe it's too ethnic. Hand us that fan over there," she said to the seamstress standing beside a worktable where the accessories were laid out.

The fan was huge, made of long white ostrich feathers. It was given to the model and Miss Lacey stepped back to view the ensemble. The showiness of the feathers fought with the busy floral pattern and overshadowed the jacket. I was sure Miss Lacey was going to take it away, but she continued to hem and haw.

Maybe she thought the frills would make the jacket more palatable to buyers, but she was killing the effect.

"Maybe just a small folding fan," I ventured.

was hoping to run into Miss Wong, but she's not due to be fitted until Monday."

"Yes, he seems to be quite a fan."

Miss Lacey chuckled. "I showed him the magazine and newspaper pictures you gave me. He was very pleased. He asked me to tell you to stop by his office at the end of your shift."

My pulse quickened. I fidgeted as the seamstress pinned the chiffon. Everything was working out just as I'd planned. Miss Lacey had praised me. Mr. Haber was pleased. This evening, then: It was the perfect opportunity to ask him to place me in the Displays Department.

I hurried through clocking out and getting my handbag, hoping to arrive at Mr. Haber's office before all the office personnel left for the night. I hadn't forgotten the accusing look Miss Buckner had given me when she saw me with the petty cash — as if I had been doing something untoward, soliciting favors from Mr. Haber.

Despite my rushing, most of the office doors were closed by the time I arrived in the personnel suite. A couple of people headed toward the elevators, and Mr. Haber's secretary was pulling her handbag out of a drawer.

"Oh, Miss Lester, Mr. Haber asked to see me," I said.

"He's on a call. Wait over there." She pointed to a chair against the wall before she moved to Mr. Haber's door. She tapped on it lightly, then opened it wide and pointed to me. He was holding the phone to his ear, but he raised a finger for me to wait.

"He'll be with you shortly." She shut the door before she lumbered down the hall. She glanced over her shoulder once. The purse of her lips sent a prickle over me.

At least ten minutes passed before Mr. Haber came out and held the door open for me. "Come in, Ruby."

I passed into the office. The late-afternoon sun streamed across the paneled room, giving it an orangey cast.

"So, you got my message." The door closed with a firm click behind me.

"I did, sir. When I got fitted today for the show." I glanced around, uncertain where to stand. Although the desk was as well-ordered as before, the two chairs facing it were loaded with files and books.

He released me then and backed away, his hands in the air again. A smear of blood stained his fingertips. "Now wait a minute," he huffed, trying to catch his breath.

I scrambled off the desk and straightened up, still clutching the scissors. My knuckles were bone white around the blades. They felt like they would split. Little sparks went off in my head as I narrowed my eyes at Mr. Haber. Blood pounded in my ears, urging me to ram the shears into his chest.

"What we have here is a misunderstanding." He plucked a handkerchief from his pocket and dabbed at his forehead, wiped his fingertips. "Put those scissors down now and run along to catch your trolley." He swiped his lip and turned the handkerchief to show me the blood. His brow arched as if I had been naughty and he was now required to scold me. "Go on home, and we'll say nothing more of this little incident."

It was rush hour, and the clamor of traffic and the swell of pedestrians engulfed me on the street. Somehow, I made it onto a Yellow Car and into an empty seat near the rear.

I was shaking, and when I looked down, the scissors gleamed in my fist against the moss-green felt of my handbag. I pushed them off my lap as if I had unearthed a scorpion. They fell with a dull *thunk*, barely audible above the screech of the trolley, the blades opened in an X. With the toe of my shoe, I slid them under the seat until they were out of my sight.

I took several deep breaths and clenched my hands to stem their trembling. I had been an idiot to go up to his office. I had ignored the gut feeling, the pinprick sensation, the secretary's glance.

A wave of hot shame rolled over me.

I should've known better, but I had just wanted . . .

I could still feel the hard metal blades in my fist. The bursting rage. I'd almost stabbed him. What would've happened then? My head pounded with the thought of the trouble that would've caused. There would've been more blood. I could've killed him. I would've been arrested.

*But I didn't do it. I didn't.* I hadn't gone off the rails. I closed my eyes and released a long breath.

Ma's and Ba's faces leaped into my head. Their mortification the afternoon Mrs. Kuen had reported on me. A lump of air lodged in my throat. I tried to swallow it down.

*Nothing happened*, I told myself. The creep had made a pass at me, and I'd bitten his lip. It hadn't hurt him any more than a slap would've. The whole incident had lasted no more than a minute. I hadn't even dropped my handbag.

Nothing had happened to him. Or to me.

*We'll say nothing more.*

# 18

I was still in a daze when I passed the Plaza on my way home. Then I heard a deep guttural voice.

"Muchacha!"

I jumped and my head snapped around. A Mexican man loitering against the wrought iron fence pointed across the street to the Lugo House.

Mrs. Kuen was leaning out a second-floor window, waving her arm. "Come up," she called to me.

I stared up at her, bewildered, as a cold sweat surfaced under my arms. *How does she already know?*

When I didn't move, she called out again. "I want to show you something."

I was being irrational. She couldn't know what had happened because I had just left Formann's.

I crossed the street and went into the building. Mrs. Kuen was the last person I wanted to see, but it seemed there was no way to avoid her. I paused in the stairwell to smooth my dress, my hair, my face. I didn't want any sign of what had happened to mark me. My hands shook and I pumped them several times before I went up.

Upstairs was the room that served as both the church and the classroom. Mrs. Kuen stood at the front, beside a piano positioned near the window.

"Look what arrived yesterday." She laid a hand on the upper case. "I saw you passing and thought you might like to see this."

It was a small walnut upright piano with a round swiveling stool. I moved up the aisle between the benches that lined the room.

"It's lovely." I wondered if she was going to ask me to play for Sunday services. We had attended church a couple of times before Mrs. Kuen came to report on me. Since then, we hadn't been back. And, as far as I knew, she hadn't visited Ma to encourage us to return. Had enough time

passed without gossip that she could risk bringing us into the fold?

"Yes. Isn't it?" Mrs. Kuen stroked the wood like a fond mother ruffling her child's hair. "Why don't you sit down and try it out?"

I wanted so badly to get home, but it would've been too odd to refuse. I went around to the stool and took a seat, my arms folded against my middle as I tried to think of what to play. "'T'ain't Nobody's Business If I Do" sprang to mind first, but instead I took up "What a Friend We Have in Jesus," playing it with slow, heavy fingering. Like a dirge. From the corner of my eye, I could see Mrs. Kuen clasp her hands, her grip tightening as I played.

When I hit the final note, she wasn't smiling. "You played that well. I can see the lessons helped you."

I nodded. I was being churlish, but I couldn't seem to help it.

"Even though those lessons did not last long," she added.

I turned on the stool to face her, girding myself.

"I've heard that your ba has retained the services of a matchmaker for you."

I sat very still and held my tongue. I didn't want to talk about this. Not now, and not with her.

"And that there are some very good prospective suitors for you to choose from. Even one or two from San Francisco." She regarded me pleasantly, as if we were discussing what hymn to play next. Her lips thinned out into something that wasn't quite a smile as she waited for me to reply.

"Choose?" The word burst out of me, weighted with bitterness. "When you're forced to choose something you don't want, it's not really a choice then, is it?"

Mrs. Kuen moved to the window, and her gaze shifted down to the street. "I've seen you and James Wong walking past the Plaza a couple of times."

*James.* A flush rose up the back of my neck. He hadn't liked that I'd taken the job at Formann's. If he heard about what happened . . .

She turned back to me. "I went to see your mother this morning. She mentioned that you two have gotten friendly. She seemed pleased about it."

I imagined Mrs. Kuen dropping by the shop under the guise of paying a social visit, innocently mentioning to Ma that she'd seen me with James.

"I must tell you that I'm surprised your mother permits you to go around with boys." She tucked her lips together, which made her look so schoolmarmish and so much older than she was. I knew what was going through her mind — that she had saved my reputation, and here I was running loose again already.

"Now, James is a very fine boy, but he is going to college in the fall." She flashed the false smile again. "It would be much more prudent for you to accept one of the matches from up north."

I began to shake my head. No. No, it was none of her business. No, I wouldn't talk about this with her.

"And I advise you to do it quickly." She came back to the piano and leaned her head down, lowering her voice. "There's always the risk of your past indiscretions being discovered. Even if this *friendship* between you and James Wong were to carry on while he attends college, having a steady suitor is not enough to protect you from your moral transgressions. In fact, it's this kind of friendship that will cause you to . . ." She blinked several times as if searching for the right word. ". . . to *falter*. Especially since you've already shown a weakness in how you conduct yourself."

She was calling me immoral, saying I had no control over myself. Heat charged through me, anger and shame all mixed up. My mind wheeled to Mr. Haber again. Was that my fault?

I couldn't think about this. Any of this.

"It will be years before a boy like James is ready to seriously consider marriage." Mrs. Kuen paused, but it seemed to me that she was pressing me, waiting for me to say something.

I closed my eyes, trying to draw up some words. "We just take walks and go to the movies."

"I understand that dating is the way of American young people, but no Chinese man will marry a girl who goes around with boys."

"I'm American."

Mrs. Kuen shook her head. "Only you see yourself as American," she said. "One foot cannot step on two boats. You're Chinese. Particularly in *their* eyes."

I hated what she was saying. And yet there was no counterargument for me to give.

"As new arrivals in this land" — she gripped her hands together and leaned in urgently — "for us to be accepted, we must work harder and behave better."

Just keep our heads down, do what we're told, stay in the shadows. That was what she meant.

"You're young, so you may not know this, but in the past — and truly, even now — we've been scapegoats for problems beyond our control, like economic troubles. We've suffered all sorts of hostilities — anti-Chinese unions, boycotts against our services, immigration restrictions. We're blocked from owning property and pushed out to the depressed area of the city."

Her agitation grew as she listed the indignities, but then she inhaled and pressed her lips together as if trying to compose herself.

"In spite of all that, we've begun to make progress. Look here at our neighborhood."

# 19

## APRIL 1924

After that drive with Russell to see the Hollywoodland sign, I couldn't stop thinking about him. I was restless, anxious, yearning to spend time with him. Piano lessons were a strain, knowing he was waiting for me outside First Methodist. As soon as the lessons were finished, I would hustle out and jump into the Model T. He said he wanted to take me to the beach, where we could dip in the waves or foxtrot in a dance hall on the boardwalk. But I was expected home, so we could only drive a block past Chinatown, to the railyard, where we spent five or ten minutes necking before I ran back to the store.

My hunger to be with him made me grow bolder. One Saturday afternoon, I told Ma that I had to go to the library to work on a school report, a lie that didn't even make me flinch. It was especially warm that day; the sun cooked my face and arms as I walked to the corner of Sunset and Spring where Russell was waiting for me. We headed north on Sunset all the way to the Hollywoodland development again, this time to see the house that his father was building for Irene. Russell played tour guide as we sipped from a flask. The gin burned my throat but then spread through my body, melting me against the seat and softening my nervous excitement.

The house was wood and stucco, two stories with a steeply pitched roof and tall windows of diamond-shaped panes. It was the largest one on the street — French Normandy style according to Russell, since all the houses had to be of European design — and close to the front of the development because Irene didn't drive and wanted quick access to the Red Car.

The yard was still just a scrubby lot. Russell pulled around to the back. "The workmen leave around lunchtime on Saturdays," he explained as we got out. Near the back door, he picked up a large rock. "The key," he said dramatically, twirling it on its metal ring before he unlocked the door.

We entered through the kitchen, which was nearly completed — the cabinets, counters, sink and range already installed. The air was stale with a closed-up feeling, but it was cooler inside than out. Russell pulled the flask from his jacket and took a long pull, then offered it to me. Already feeling a little jellied from the nips I'd taken on the drive, I shook my head.

He led me through the first floor. The strong scent of raw lumber wafted from the flooring and the dark-stained panels that covered the lower half of the walls. I couldn't believe the amount of space for just two people. I knew that people lived like this, but even in San Francisco, everyone I knew had lived in the tenements or in the back of the family business.

We mounted the steps. The stuffy heat of the second floor enveloped us on the landing.

"This bathroom is the showpiece of the whole place." Russell pushed a door open. "Irene wanted it finished first."

Pink tile covered most of the walls, except where there was a lead-paned window. I'd never seen a window inside a bathroom. The sun slanted onto the white-penny-tile floor and gleamed off the nickel-plated fixtures of the claw-foot tub, grandly positioned under the window. I threw Russell a baffled look when I saw a metal hose with an apparatus resting on an out-rigged stand near the faucets.

"Take it," he said, "then turn on the faucet."

I picked it up and rotated the faucet. Water spurted out like rain. I wagged it around, streaming the lines of water out like a ribbon. "Nifty!" I twitched it in Russell's direction.

"Hey!" He put his hands up, but the water spattered him. He dropped the flask and lunged for the sprayer head. We wrestled over it, laughing as we tried to keep the spray of water toward the tub. Russell dodged and caught me around the waist. Even as I laughed and wriggled, a palpable throb began inside me. I twisted in his arms and brandished the sprayer over my shoulder to sprinkle him again, but he managed to turn it on me. The cold water made me gasp.

"Turn if off! Turn it off!" I cried.

Russell bent us over as he shut the water off and let the hose drop into the tub. It landed with a *thunk*, and after that, only our heavy exhalations were audible as we caught our breath after laughing so hard.

We were both more than damp, and my shirt clung to my chest. Russell's arms were still wrapped around me. I shifted around to face him. Drips of water marked his cheek. I started to wipe them, but I went still as his gaze ran over my lips, down my neck, to the button at the top of my blouse. He pulled me against him, and the heat of his body made an ache stretch from the pit of my belly clear down to my knees.

We were kissing then. Softly at first, lips and tongues teasing at each other. Then the kissing turned harder, more intense.

We moved together away from the tub and lowered ourselves onto the floor. The tile was hard against my knees as I straddled him. He clasped the backs of my thighs, and my skirt shifted up as I worked myself against him. Everything fell away except that deep, deep ache.

Until a short shriek cut through the air.

My head jerked up. Irene stood on the landing outside the bathroom, shock scrawled across her face. Pierre, her fiancé, was behind her with his jaw fallen open, but he swiftly stepped out of sight.

"Russell!" Irene said in a horrified voice.

Russell pushed me off. I wrenched down my skirt as I scrambled off to the side of the room, out of Irene's sight, hot with embarrassment and the cut-off yearning that was still right there.

Russell bounded up and closed the door with a quiet click. He kept one hand pressed against it as if he was afraid Irene was going to push in.

"Russell!" Irene said again through the door, her voice low but quaking.

Neither Russell nor I moved. He kept his head tucked down, didn't even glance my way.

"I'm telling you, Russell. You get her out of here now and send her back home!"

*Her.*

I suddenly felt numb, but my body was chilled. The cold dampness of my clothes went straight to my bones. I began to tremble.

The studio lot was several blocks away. I grew even more excited as we approached the entrance. The street side of the lot was fronted by a long clapboard building that stretched on and on. Several people loitered on the sidewalk. Russell had once mentioned that people lined up outside hoping to be cast as extras. I scanned their faces, anxious that he might be among them, but thankfully he wasn't.

Some of the folks noticed Anna May and greeted her with fawning smiles, addressing her as Miss Wong. She smiled and nodded back as she walked by, keeping one hand tucked casually in the pocket of her suit. She seemed perfectly at ease with the attention. Again, I was amazed at how changeable she was.

The guard opened the paned glass door for us and tipped his cap at Anna May.

Anna May dropped off her contract with the receptionist, then said, "We'll slip through some of the back stages on the way to the commissary. I'm sure they'll be shooting something."

We left through the lot's side exit and walked a short distance to a huge warehouse. The inside was a complete contrast to the stark exterior. The ceiling was made of some kind of translucent material so the whole warehouse was bright. Ropes and pulleys and electric lights were lashed amid the rafters. Floor lights and other pieces of equipment were scattered around sets that were sectioned off into cubbyholes. It was like walking through a playhouse; we passed a deserted living room with a settee beside a fireplace, then a fake patio, then an artist's loft.

All the bustle surrounded a bathroom arrangement with a claw-foot tub. Two cameras and several lights on stands were pointed at the set, and a group of people buzzed behind them. I caught sight of a man dressed in a tuxedo and a pink-robed woman with heavily kohled eyes. Both their faces were caked with greasepaint. We stole past, keeping well out of the way of the film crew, then went by even more sets before we came out the other end of the warehouse.

"Hope you don't mind that we didn't stop to watch," Anna May said. "I'm so hungry, I could eat a horse."

It was on the early side for lunch, and most of the small tables in the commissary

Frances and I turned to see what had gotten her attention. A man and a woman had entered. The man had his arm around the woman's waist as he led her to a table in the corner.

For once, Anna May seemed to lose control over her face. The liveliness went out, and she turned her back to the couple. Frances placed her hand on Anna May's forearm and squeezed. "Come on, dear," she said in a soothing tone, "let's have that table over here."

I glanced at the couple as I followed Anna May and Frances to a table in the corner. The woman was the actress Blanche Sweet, I was fairly certain.

Anna May stared down into her coffee cup. We hadn't spent much time together, but this was the first time I'd seen her lose that perfect composure. I wondered what it was all about.

Frances sipped at her coffee and peered uneasily at Anna May, but then she spoke to me. "Ruby, you have a lovely figure and beautiful hair. You really don't want to be in the pictures? I'm working on a new scenario. I could use you as an extra, one of the harem girls."

Although I knew she meant it as a compliment, I couldn't help but wince. Modeling bathing suits in a roomful of ladies was one thing, but having my image as a woman of ill repute played over and over for crowds of people would be another thing altogether. "I'm no actress."

"Well, it's unusual to meet someone who's not champing at the bit to get into the movies. Is it true that the Chinese believe cameras and photographs take possession of the soul?" She turned to Anna May. "Didn't you mention that in an interview, dear?"

Frances was trying to draw her out, but Anna May only answered with a washed-out half smile. I glanced back at the couple near the window. Her change in mood had something to do with them. They each had looked our way, but Anna May kept her back to them.

"I'm so looking forward to next month's premiere night for *The Thief of Bagdad*. Everyone is." Frances patted Anna May's hand. Whatever was happening with Anna May, Frances seemed to understand. She turned back to me. "It's not because of your soul, is it? The reason why you don't want to be in pictures?"

"No," I laughed, "I don't believe that, though my ma does." Which was possibly why she hadn't pushed me to get my photograph made like Auntie Matchmaker had been nagging about.

"Well, tell me about your family's store," Frances said. "What do you sell?"

"It's called Chan's Art Emporium. It's on Apablasa Street, just off Alameda. We specialize in Chinese art pieces and furniture. My father's overseas now on a buying trip for stock."

"I haven't been slumming in Chinatown for some time now. Seems like when I get that way it's only to have a quick bite. Next time I'm there, I'll have to take a march around. I'm always on the scout for story inspiration and shooting locations."

I flinched at the *slumming* comment, but the truth was our businesses benefited from the tourism. White people showed up clutching pamphlets that promised views of opium dens, joss houses, and real Chinese families in their homes. They left after spending money on our wares, food, and services.

"I thought your job was to write the scripts," I said. "You also pick where they're filmed?"

"Oh, yes, I have a hand in everything. Scene setting, how the actors move, title cards, camera effects. I envision the whole movie in my head and get it all down in the continuity script."

A waiter came to the table to take our order. There was a choice of pot roast or salmon patties.

"What's the sauce on the salmon?" Frances asked.

As the waiter and Frances discussed the menu, Anna May leaned toward me. "Do you mind terribly if we don't stay? I seem to have lost my appetite and I don't think I can sit still to watch you two eat a whole meal."

I'd never tried pot roast, so I was disappointed, but she obviously needed to get away. "Of course. I don't mind."

"Frances, do you mind eating alone?" Anna May asked her.

Frances waved her hand. "Don't worry about me. I've got plenty of work to keep me company." She patted the stack of folders she'd set on the table.

"About what?"

"Anything. Are you excited about Shanghai Chic?"

The memory of Mr. Haber forcing himself against me heaved into my mind.

"I am." Bile was threatening to push up into my throat, but I stoppered it and tried to sound enthusiastic. "I don't care so much about the modeling part, but it's like you said — such a fine chance to highlight Chinese styles."

"Yes, slumming and Orientalism are so popular now." She rolled her eyes. "Might as well make some good use of it. You know, I ran into that Mr. Haber today. He came down to the fitting room and mooned around the whole time I was getting pinned. He gives me the creeps. You'd better watch out for him."

I strained for a response, but nothing came out. When she turned to look at me, I turned toward the window. Squat buildings, telegraph poles, and palms scrolled by.

She nudged me. "Ruby?"

I tried to fix my face in a smile, but her eyes didn't let up.

"What did he do?"

I flicked my hand as if it was nothing to bother about.

"Tell me," she persisted.

"He tried to kiss me," I said lightly, even though my tongue felt like it was sticking in my mouth. "I was stupid. I went up to his office to ask to be moved to the Displays Department and he . . ." I strangled on the rest and waved my hand again.

Anna May's dark eyes bore into me, waiting.

"Don't worry. There was a pair of scissors on his desk. As soon as I grabbed them, he backed right off." I chuckled, but it came out flat.

Her mouth fell open and she grabbed my hand. "If it was so bad that you had to fight him off with scissors, you should report him."

"No! It was nothing. Nothing happened." I pulled my hand back and crossed my arms. "Report him to who, anyway? He's the personnel director. Besides, I can't lose my job before the show. It was my idea! And my family needs the money from the pieces Formann's will be renting from the store."

She gazed at me. With sympathy? Disappointment? I couldn't tell.

"Listen, I really want to see the show through," I said. "I'll probably quit afterward."

Anna May exhaled a long, exasperated breath that sounded like a punctured tire. "It's not right. But I guess I know a little about that kind of thing."

As gorgeous as Anna May was, she'd probably dealt with her share of handsy men in the picture business. I thought back to her reaction when she saw that couple at the movie studio.

"What happened back in the commissary?" I asked, keen to shift the conversation away from myself.

Anna May dropped her gaze to her lap.

"You don't have to tell me, but you seemed so rattled after that couple showed up . . ."

"It was Mickey Neilan and Blanche Sweet." She gnawed at her lip, then let out another tremulous sigh. "I had a thing going with Mickey. It started when I was working on *Bits of Life* in San Francisco. He was the director."

I couldn't hide my surprise. My hand flew up to smother the small noise that came out of my mouth. *Bits of Life* had been about three years back. She would've been around my age then, and that fella had looked well past thirty.

"Well, we fell in love. He was going to divorce his wife and marry me. We were going to get married in Tijuana. His buddies talked him out of it — reminded him that the marriage wouldn't be legal once we crossed back into the States. And that his career would be ruined, of course."

"That vile law," I said. "As if it's a taint for a white person to marry one of us." Yet another way to make us into second-class citizens even if we'd been born here.

"I thought he walked on air." Her voice was just above a whisper. "But he broke it off. He divorced his wife anyway and married Blanche a couple of years ago." She closed her eyes and pressed her fingertips to her temples. "I'm glad now that it didn't happen, but I hate that I was taken in by such a cad."

*Taken in.* A lump rose in my throat. I tried to think of something to say, but the moment passed as our streetcar drew up to our stop on Main Street.

We hopped off the trolley and walked to Ferguson Alley to a building I remembered seeing before. *Jerry's Joynt* was painted on the side, along with *World Famous Spareribs. Chop Suey. Chinese Dishes.* Iron grillwork shielded the windows, and posters and advertisements were plastered on the brick near the door. I had assumed it was a spot for tourists and was surprised that Anna May frequented the place.

The lower three quarters of the windows had been papered over, so the restaurant was dim and cool. The stench of stale cigarette smoke and fry oil was thick in the air. Three or four of the tables were occupied. Anna May and I were the only women. The other customers were white men, and they craned their heads to gawp at us — mostly Anna May in her unusual suit — as we crossed to the rear and slid into one of the sticky booths that lined the walls. It was a far cry from the airy, clean commissary of the picture studio.

Anna May drummed her fingers against the table. She leaned forward and muttered, "You know what? We need a drink."

Despite Prohibition — and it not even being one o'clock in the afternoon — I knew she wasn't talking about soda or tea. I wasn't all that shocked. My parents generally had nothing to do with spirits as far as I knew, but Ba always managed to find some at the New Year. And Russell had introduced me to his flask on more than one occasion.

Anna May motioned to the waiter. He came straightaway. She curled her finger for him to bend down. "Billy, do me a favor and bring us a couple of jiggers," she said in his ear. She dug in her purse and brought out four quarters, which she slipped into his hand. "I guess you'd better splash some orange juice over it."

Billy slipped the coins into his pocket and straightened up. "And what to eat, Anna May?"

Anna May ordered her sardine sandwich and I asked for egg salad. After Billy left for the kitchen, Anna May slumped back in her seat. She seemed so damn sad, I figured she must be thinking about Mickey Neilan again.

"I know how you feel," I said. "About being taken in."

She lifted an eyebrow at me. "Do you?"

"The reason I left school had to do with a . . ." I was at a loss as what to call Russell. "A boyfriend." That was how I'd thought of him, I supposed. Before the worst of it. "Sort of. I was mad about him too."

Billy was back at the table, depositing two glasses of orange juice with chunks of ice. I took a sip. The coldness of it was bracing, but otherwise it tasted bright and sweet with a bitter kick to it. I took a long swallow.

"So, this sort-of-boyfriend, who was he?" Anna May swirled her glass, the ice clinking.

"His name is Russell. He's a senior at Polytech." I took another sip. I told her about the piano lessons with Irene, how he showed up that day, the rush he gave me. The gin in the juice seemed to loosen my tongue.

It was strange to talk about Russell, about matters that came close to the heart. Holding back our feelings was the Chinese way, and although I seemed to have no problem letting out my anger, I wasn't used to talking about tender emotions.

Anna May seemed to understand this. She didn't press me to get too personal, but she encouraged me to keep talking with tiny dips of her head and prompting comments: "And then?" "Oh, my." "I can imagine!"

With her wide, round eyes on me, I kept talking, leaving out only a few things: the time that Russell had shown me that magazine photo of her and the details of our more intimate moments.

"Well, what happened in the end?" By now, the sandwiches had arrived, and she took another bite. All her misery had fallen away. "How did it break up?"

I reached for my glass and took the last swallow of melted ice. The shame was too painful to explain. I didn't understand it myself. I wasn't sure how I'd let everything get so muddled.

"His family found out about us — his sister and his mother, at least — and they didn't like it. We had to stop seeing each other."

"You mean *he* had to stop?"

I nodded.

"He's got a matchmaker from San Francisco working on my case as well."

"Oh yes, my father tried that a few years ago — made inquiries, anyway. Nothing came of it, but he's always telling me I need to get a good Chinese husband." She smacked her tongue in exasperation. Then her eyes widened. "Ruby, you know that if a woman marries a noncitizen, the law says she loses her American citizenship!"

"I know, but it's not going to happen." Ba couldn't make me get married. I was American, and I had choices. Didn't I? "I'd run away first. Move out, I mean." My second glass was empty, and the egg and mayonnaise began to feel heavy in my stomach. My whole body was heavy. The conversation was depressing me. "What time is it? I should get back home. I have some things to do before I meet up with James tonight." My head was foggy and thick. A nap was what I needed.

"James? You mean my brother?" Surprise crossed her face.

"Yes. Didn't he tell you?" I grinned. "We've gotten friendly since that trip to the department store when you bought him the typewriter."

"No. He's not mentioned it." Her lips twitched ever so slightly. "Don't tell me your parents are eyeing Jimmy as your future husband."

"No!" The room seemed to bounce. I could feel my neck turning splotchy with the shame of Ma's scheme. "I told you, I'm not getting married. James and I are just friends." The heat spread up to my face. Why was I lying? We had gone well past the *friends* stage, necking and all, but the cool way she had asked the question got my back up. It was none of her business what was going on between James and me.

Anna May leaned back and began to drum her fingers on the table again. "Jimmy's starting college at the end of the summer. He'll be meeting all kinds of people. And . . . well, he's not going to get married anytime soon."

I couldn't believe what I was hearing. Did she not think I was good enough for her brother? It could've been Mrs. Kuen talking.

"But mostly . . . well, the two of you wouldn't be very well-suited to each other." Anna May cocked her head again

"What?" Miss Lacey pressed her chest as if she were having an attack. "What's happened?"

Mr. Haber's gaze scoured the room until his eyes fixed on me. I flinched, my insides crawling, but I stood stock still. "She has been completely unprofessional, that's what's happened. After all our efforts. After the advertisement we placed in the *Times*!"

"She's supposed to start and finish the show!" Miss Lacey cried. "Why isn't she coming?"

"Because she's a scheming, deceitful, unscrupulous Chinese . . ." Mr. Haber's chest heaved and hawed like a bellows. "This theme was her idea and then she can't even be bothered to show up!"

The scorn in his voice made my blood rise. I gripped my hands together and pressed them against my middle. My feet burned to walk out.

But the show hadn't been Anna May's idea. It had been mine. And if I left now, wouldn't that be everything terrible that Mr. Haber said about us?

"Hang it all, that's three outfits!" Miss Lacey raced over to a rack and began to rifle through the ones she'd tagged for Anna May.

Why hadn't she come? It had to be something more than *she couldn't be bothered.*

"We don't have time to pull anyone from the floor!" Miss Lacey snatched a black embroidered Mandarin coat off the rack and thrust it at a girl. "Gay, you take this one and go for a third run." She pulled down two more outfits. "Lucille and Esther, I think these will fit you. There's no time to try them on now. After your second dresses, run back here and see if they'll fit." She spun to address the seamstresses. "Be ready to do anything you can to make them work. Everyone, line up! We must head upstairs. Miss Adams will be waiting!"

The girls muttered a few more disparaging comments as they scuttled to get in order. The hostility in the room was thick. My throat was furry with it, but I swallowed it down and took my place, wishing I were invisible.

Miss Lacey looked us over once more before we crowded into the service elevator and lined up again in the corridor outside the pavilion. Mr. Haber opened the

Her hands splayed out on her desk, and she leaned forward on them, waiting, daring me to argue.

Mr. Haber's scissors. The three dollars he gave me. They flickered into my mind like the loose end of a movie reel.

My armpits were clammy with sweat. A vise clamped around my chest, my heart thrashing inside. The police. She had me over a barrel. More than she knew. After what had happened with Russell, his parents threatening to charge me, even a false accusation was too much to bring to our home. My face was hot, so hot that I thought my head would burst.

There was nothing to do but leave.

# 23

JULY 1924

Ma sent me to Sam Kee's with our sheets a week and a half later. I was wary about running into Anna May, but luckily James was at the counter, and the huge grin he cracked tempered my uneasiness.

"I'm sorry I haven't come around to see you," he said as I hoisted my basket up. He glanced toward the passage to the workroom before he caught my hand on the counter and gave it a squeeze. "I've wanted to, but Papa's had me busy. One of the big wringers has been giving us problems, so we had to take it apart to fix it, and that left us to work double-time with the other one. How'd the fashion show go last week?"

"It went fine." I forced a smile. There was no way I was going to explain to him what'd happened. "And I quit the store."

"You quit?" His face brightened. I felt a twinge of guilt for lying to him.

"I think I learned everything I needed there. Now I want to focus on helping Mr. Lew with the shop." I had given Ma the same line, the first explanation that had popped into my head. Unfortunately, because I'd said that, I couldn't go out and start looking for another job.

But I didn't have the heart to start working again anyway. Not *out there*, where I would have to face the likes of Miss Buckner and Mr. Haber. I was wrung out from everything that had happened, the whole summer, everyone, even my own family. I had no energy for anything except doing the housework and shop work. I couldn't even think about what would happen once Ba came home.

"How's Anna May?" I asked, ready to change the subject. "I heard she was sick."

James shook his head. "Not that I know of. She's fine. Out and about, as always."

"But she missed the fashion show because she was sick."

"She didn't mention it." He frowned as he dumped the laundry on the counter and began counting the sheets. "I don't recall her being sick. But then she hasn't been around much."

Anna May hadn't been sick.

When Mr. Haber had announced that she was ill, I'd had a nagging feeling that it wasn't true. But then why had she cut out on the show? The last time we'd talked about it, she'd seemed happy to be part of it. To shine the spotlight on the culture, she'd said.

"She's been running around busy with movie work, getting ready for the big fancy premiere on Thursday." James made a face. "Buying shoes and getting dresses tailored."

Had she skipped the fashion show because of me? Because she thought I was trying to weasel in with James?

"Will *you* be going to the premiere?" I asked, keeping up my end of the conversation even as my mind was reeling in another direction. Maybe I wasn't good enough for James, but ruining my show after all the work I'd put into it was a kick in the teeth.

"No. The tickets are five dollars," James said. "Anna May does have a ticket for Papa, but he's balking about going."

"Is it because of her part?" The scanty costume, the duplicitous Mongol slave character. All those awful things Mr. Haber said about us came rushing back to me.

James's expression clouded, and he began to pile all the sheets into one of the laundry's baskets. "No one's had the nerve to show him any of the photos of her costume, but he's heard about it."

Anna May had said her ba was irked about the picture. All that talk about our families. We had traded confidences. I had told her about Ba and the matchmaking, and she'd twisted it all around. And then to bunk off the show when she knew what it meant to me — that was worse than the fact that I'd been fired. She'd used my confidences against me.

"He'd be nuts to miss out on something like that." My words were airy, with no hint of the humiliation and spite stirring just under the surface. "You should talk him into going."

James grimaced, then jutted his chin toward the open door. "You can talk to him yourself."

The clop and clatter of the horse and wagon sounded from the street as James's ba drew up in front of the store. James headed outside. I grabbed my empty basket and followed him.

"Papa, this is Ruby. Her ba took over Mr. Lew's shop." He moved to the rear of the wagon and began unloading empty baskets from the bed.

I shielded my eyes against the sun as I greeted Mr. Wong, perched on the wagon seat, reins in hand. He peered down at me from beneath his stocking cap. His blue Tang jacket was covered in dust.

"Ah, yes. I heard about him." Mr. Wong nodded. "And he's gone home for the summer."

I nodded. I was pleased to know that James must've spoken about me to him. And yet there was still that uneasy, vindictive churning inside me. Anna May ought to know what it felt like — to be humiliated the way I had been. She thought she was above it all. With her fame and her rave reviews and her new production company, she thought she no longer had to care what other people thought of her.

Of us. She thought she was immune to shame.

"James and I were just talking about Anna May's new movie," I said. "He says you're not going to the premiere."

Mr. Wong tugged at the standing collar of his jacket. "I've no time for that sort of thing."

"But the movie's getting the most marvelous reviews and the papers are full of the premiere," I gushed. "It's going to be at Grauman's Egyptian Theatre. They're decorating the front of it to look like Bagdad and they're going to perfume the theater with scents of Arabia!"

Mr. Wong had the same flying-back eyebrows as James. He arched one of them up, which only encouraged me to keep laying it on.

"And they're calling the movie *the greatest thing that ever has been put on screen*." I was pushing my luck, but I couldn't seem to stop. "I read that they've used all kinds of new trick shots to make Douglas Fairbanks fly on a rug and climb a rope that stands up on its own. It cost over a million dollars to make the picture." I flashed an innocent smile at Mr. Wong. "Your own daughter, in one of the biggest movies ever made! Golly, I wouldn't miss it for anything."

Mr. Wong pulled off his cap. His hair-line had retreated to the back of his head. When he rubbed his scalp, I knew I had struck a note with him.

It was family, after all.

# 24

On Friday I headed back to Sam Kee to collect our laundry. Along the way, I picked up the *Times* from a newsboy, then set my basket right down on the sidewalk and opened the paper. I found the write-up about *The Thief of Bagdad* on page nine.

*Film Banquet is Dazzling.* Three long columns raved about the opening and the feature itself. Four or five paragraphs were devoted to detailing the theater design — Oriental deities, minarets, hanging rugs, burning incense. It was described as an Arabian Nights fantasy, with dancing harem girls gracing the aisles, usherettes in long veils, and the orchestra dressed in turbans and sheik costumes.

I could picture it in my mind — the flock of white actresses and musicians with brown greasepaint and heavily lined eyes, the garish costumes, the hodgepodge of real and imagined cultures lumped together. As perplexing as the depictions must've been, I would've loved to see such a huge spectacle in person.

I read that introductions had been made for the whole cast, including *a number of them Oriental.* That pleased me, and despite my grudge toward Anna May, I swelled when the reviewer commented that, to his mind, she had done the *best bits of acting as the intriguing Chinese girl.* I couldn't wait to see the movie. Fifty cents would be a lot to pay for a matinee, but the Egyptian Theatre was new, a lavish movie palace, and it had an exclusive on the picture.

At the laundry, Mary Wong, one of the younger siblings, was working the counter. After she handed over my packets of clean laundry, I asked her if James was home, and she told me he was out back.

I lugged my basket around the side of the building and found him sitting on an upturned pail, a grease-streaked rag in his hand. He smiled up at me.

"What are you doing?" I set my basket down. "I smell vinegar."

"Cleaning these nuts and bolts from the wringer. Now the other one is acting up."

"I came by to pick up the laundry."

"I figured, what with the basket and all those packets."

I laughed, and he asked me to wait a minute so he could walk me home. He dumped the vinegar out and went into the workroom with the hardware.

That was when I heard it.

"You have no decorum! No shame!" A deep voice rose above the shuddering of the wash drum agitators that floated out to the yard from the workroom. "Being an actress is low enough, but no girl in China would show herself like that!"

The second-floor windows were thrown open. Anna May stood in view just beyond a sheer curtain, and I knew the voice was her ba's.

"I'm not like those girls and never will be!" Anna May wasn't shouting, but her voice was firm.

"That man promised me he would guard your reputation," her ba thundered.

"Instead, he dresses you like a — a wanton!" He moved into the frame of the window. His arms flew in the air. "Ha! *Dresses* is the wrong word — strips you down, puts your flesh on display for the pleasure of the white devils."

"It's acting, Papa!"

"Don't you see how these people already think of us? Like villains, no morals!"

I cringed as he boiled on.

"You reinforce it by playing those parts!"

"But that's all they offer me." Anna May sounded so frustrated, I felt a twinge in my chest.

"And you take it! Like a dog eating measly leftovers they throw at you."

"All I can do is take what I can get and do the best job that I can until I can get another part. A better part. Then a better one after that. It's happening, Papa. Already happening. We're finding the money for my production company! Don't you want us to do better?"

"Better? They'll never accept you. This won't amount to anything! You should have at least finished school. Gone to college like your sister!"

*future. The arrangement would be beneficial to all.*

Mr. Lew frowned. "Good for business, yes. But the men here need girls to marry. What about that matchmaker?" he asked Ma.

Ma's face twisted. "She sent a letter last week. The suitors are eager to set a meeting. But I think that should wait until Ruby's ba is home . . ."

"I'm not getting married!" I snapped. "To anyone, anywhere!"

Taken aback at my sharp tone, Mr. Lew tucked his chin. Maybe he meant to be helpful in trying to keep me at home, but his old-fashioned expectations were revealing themselves like a sagging slip.

The memory of James in the alley sidled into my mind. What was he going to ask me? It wasn't possible, was it?

Mr. Lew raised the letter to his face again. "He also wants to know if you've sent the photograph of Ruby that he has been waiting for."

Ma stepped away from the crate. "Tea?" she asked Mr. Lew. Then, without waiting for his answer, she said to me, "Leave that and help with the tea."

I followed her to the back room and crumpled onto a stool. A widowed merchant! It was too unbelievable. Ba was bluffing. He wouldn't really try to make me go through with getting married when he knew how interested I was in the shop.

Ma pumped the faucet at the sink. "How is it with James?" She kept her back to me as she filled the kettle, but she didn't try to hide the gravity in her voice.

James's dark eyes came back to me. *I've been thinking. About us.* I wasn't sure how much I wanted to share. I couldn't stand it if she got into a flutter over what might turn out to be nothing.

She wiped the kettle and set it on the stove. "You've walked out with him so many times."

"Mmm." I compressed my lips.

"How many times?" She gripped the dishcloth against her midriff and wrung it absently, her knuckles white. "Four or five? That's enough to make an arrangement."

I rose and retrieved cups from the shelf. I was so very tired of this conversation.

"Do you expect that he'll ask? Will you come to an arrangement?"

If I encouraged Ma, she'd charge ahead, determined to turn a possibility into a firm reality. To her, I knew, this seemed like the simplest solution to my problems, but for me it was still a tangle. Of what I felt for James now and what I might later come to feel, of what I didn't want yet and might never want.

I shook my head.

"No? What do you mean? No, it's not going to happen? Or just no, not yet?"

"Ma! I like James, but I don't want to get married. Not yet!"

She was quick to move beside me, her hand on my arm. "You can't afford to delay. You must try with James. Your father's going to be home in five or six more weeks." She turned me to face her. "Ruby-ah, pearls don't lie on the seashore. If you want one, you must dive for it."

I scoffed and pulled away. "Like you did? With Ba? Marrying someone twice your age?"

Surprise came over her face. "Yes."

I closed my eyes and shook my head. I knew she hadn't chosen him. It had been an arranged match.

"You think I didn't want to marry your ba?" She sighed. "Why would you think that? My family sold me as a servant because they couldn't feed me." Her eyes turned dark. "My tai-tai wasn't bad to me, but the husband, he had begun to . . . bother me."

Her words ripped through me. For a moment Mr. Haber's rough, grasping hands were all over me again.

"What choice did I have? Run away to the Ladies Aid Society and rely on the white ghosts to protect me? Some people said they helped abused girls, but then you also heard that bad men raided their boardinghouse." She closed her eyes and shrugged one shoulder. I saw the young woman she must've been, scared and confused. "I knew I had to take my situation into my own hands. I found Auntie Matchmaker and she found your father for me."

"You made your arrangement with Auntie Matchmaker?" I imagined Ma at fifteen or sixteen years old, unable to read or write, searching for a matchmaker. As a mui-tsai, she wouldn't have had family or even friends to help her, so I pictured her roaming the streets and alleys of San Francisco's Chinatown on her own, timidly asking if anyone knew a matchmaker.

Ma nodded. "I was bound to work with the family until I was eighteen. But once Auntie Matchmaker found your ba for me, I told the tai-tai about the trouble with her husband. She let me go."

I was speechless. Ma, who had always been so deferential, so gentle, had found a way out of a bad situation and had executed it.

"Ma!" I moved back near her, grabbed her hand, and squeezed. "You did that on your own?"

"It was a long time ago." She shook her head as if to dismiss the past. "After Mrs. Kuen came and your ba decided you had to get married, I told him to write to Auntie Matchmaker."

I sucked in a breath. "*You* called Auntie Matchmaker for me!"

"Yes! I had to. Your ba simply intended to send you to China. Auntie Matchmaker will keep you here. At least here in America. But you still have time to steer your own future. If there's any chance that James —"

A crash sounded from the shop. Ma and I rushed to see Mr. Lew lying on the floor clutching his chest, broken porcelain scattered around him. Ma let out a strangled cry as she knelt at his side.

"Run to Hung Wong Ho's!" she shouted. "Tell the herbalist it's an emergency. Probably the heart."

# 26

Mr. Lew recuperated on a pallet in the back room for a few days until he was well enough to return to his rooming house. Ma tried to get him to stay put, but he insisted that the other bachelors in his tenement would take care of him, and the two men who supported him on either side nodded to confirm this as they exited the shop.

I shut and locked the door behind them while Ma went back to the kitchen. The crates scattered amid the dusty display furniture made my heart sink. Between helping Ma with the housework and caring for Mr. Lew, I'd managed only a little of the unpacking. The store had been closed since his attack, and already the air felt musty. The pungent scents of Mr. Lew's unwashed body and the pot-boiled astragalus-and-longan-berry tea he'd been ordered to drink four times a day seeped in from the kitchen.

I went to Ba's desk and opened the account book. The sales column for the last few months held paltry sums for curios and a few smaller pieces of furniture. Mr. Lew knew everything about the pieces, but he wasn't the most enterprising salesman. The one standout entry in the *Received* column was the seventy dollars from Formann's Department Store. I sighed, thinking back to the Shanghai Chic show. Miss Adams had complimented me on the setting. It would've been nice to have really worked with her and Miss Lacey.

I flipped back a few pages in the ledger, and my gaze fell on a pair of entries: four hundred dollars borrowed from the Chinese Benevolent Association and four hundred paid out. The *Payable To* space beside the sum was blank, but I knew it had been paid to the Blythes. My stomach turned queasy as I wondered what reason Ba had given the clan for borrowing the money, but I was also vexed that he'd paid the Blythes despite my telling him not to do it. He hadn't even asked me if their accusations were true.

I flipped the page. Ba's ship ticket, the money advanced for purchases on his trip, the rent for our building . . . A sinking feeling pulled at my chest with each entry. If the store stayed closed until Ba came home, we'd fall further into the hole.

And with only a bride price to save us.

My mind circled back to James, the boys interrupting us in the alley. He hadn't been back to see me yet, but I supposed he'd heard about Mr. Lew's illness and knew that we'd be busy taking care of him. What had he wanted to say to me that day? My pulse fluttered. I couldn't let myself wonder. I still couldn't fathom getting married to anyone. But what would I do once Ba came home? Especially if the store was in shambles.

I shut the ledger and carried it to the back.

Ma was on her knees, rolling up the pallet we'd dragged down for Mr. Lew. A pile of bedding lay beside her.

"Ma, what if we open the shop and I run it until Ba gets home?"

"You know your ba doesn't want you in front of the customers." She straightened up and reached for the broom.

"Ba didn't know that Mr. Lew would get sick and that we'd have to close the shop," I pointed out. I plopped the ledger on the table. "We have to do something. The money situation is bad."

Ma closed her eyes for a moment, then began to sweep. "Nothing to be done about it. We must wait until your ba comes home."

"But with nothing coming in for the next month, we'll be ruined! We can't let the business wash away. All the new things that Ba sent shouldn't sit around collecting dust. What about controlling our destiny? Diving for pearls?"

Ma smacked her tongue in exasperation. "That's not what I meant. I was talking about you trying harder with James."

I bristled, but it also broke my heart that Ma had such a limited view, that she thought getting married was the only solution.

"Your circumstances were different than mine," I told her. "There was no other choice for you. Girls have options now. I've worked in the store, I do the books. I know I can run it until Ba gets home."

"Doesn't matter." She stopped sweeping and thrust her chin at me. "Your ba is making plans already. You want to take a chance on his changing his mind?"

I opened my mouth to respond, but Ma cut me off.

"You like James, don't you? Focus on that. I'll talk to Mr. Lew in a few days about the store. Now, call the boys to take up the pallet and help me finish cleaning. After we're done you can take these sheets to the laundry."

Later that day, as I was about to leave with the sheets, Ma handed me a note.

"Give it to the Wong girl."

She had scrawled out Anna May's Chinese name in her childlike handwriting, but, taken by surprise, I still asked, "You mean Anna May?"

"Yes."

The awful fight I'd engineered between her and her ba was still in my mind. I eyed the note uneasily. What could Ma possibly have to say to her? If it was about James and me, she was barking up the wrong tree. "What's it about?"

"It has nothing to do with you! Go on now."

On North Figueroa Street, as I approached the laundry, I spotted James up on the flat roof. Men's shirts hung shoulder to shoulder on wash lines strung between posts under the glaring sun.

I left the basket at the foot of the staircase that clung to the side of the building. James didn't notice me as I stepped onto the roof. Watching him work in his rolled-up sleeves reminded me of my first glimpse of him a couple of months earlier. His forearms were tanned brown, hard and muscly from baseball and laundry work.

I swept my braid over my shoulder to drape onto my chest. "Hey there," I called out to James, but not too loudly. Another worker was on the far side of the roof.

James twisted around, looking up from the shirt he was hanging. He seemed surprised to see me. "Hi."

I moved closer as he finished pinning the shirt to the line and reached down for another one from the basket near his feet.

"What time are you going to be done here?" I asked. "Can we go for a soda?"

He snapped the shirt to release the wrinkles. "Nah, I don't think I can."

She traced her finger along the threading, a dreamy expression on her face. "Double cranes." Anna May raised a brow at Ma, then flicked her eyes to me. "Marriage?"

What was Ma doing?

"They're flying toward the sun." Ma's eyes skittered toward me. "Ambition."

Something warm flooded through me, a feeling I couldn't quite name.

"I've seen your picture in the newspaper. I thought of how hard you work, how much you've climbed." Ma beamed at Anna May with genuine admiration. "I wanted to offer this quilt to you before we put it in the store."

"Ma!" Now I realized what she was doing. She was going to sell the coverlet to Anna May as a way of helping me. "You can't! All your work . . ." I knew what it meant to her, the painstaking hours she'd labored over it. It could command a good price — a hundred dollars, maybe more — but it was *hers*.

"Doesn't matter, doesn't matter." Ma patted my hand. "It's just a blanket. I've already started another one."

Anna May's eyes flashed between Ma and me. "I'm so honored." She placed a hand on her chest. "I wish I could purchase it. It's exactly the type of art I'd love to collect." Then she smiled apologetically. "Unfortunately, I can't afford it right now. You see, I've put money down on a house."

"A house!" Ma gazed at Anna May with absolute awe. "Very good! Your family is moving?" She glanced at me.

Anna May shook her head. "No, just me."

Ma's expression shifted to worry. "You're going to live there alone?"

"All by myself." Anna May pulled a tight smile.

"Is it here in Chinatown?"

"No. Hollywood."

"Why not in the neighborhood?" Ma asked.

Anna May sighed and lowered her gaze to the coverlet again. I supposed she didn't want to live in a neighborhood where so many people scorned her — even her own father. But would she be any more accepted out there? I had an awful feeling, imagining her rootless and alone.

"My agents suggested I buy there. Especially since there's chatter about a new train station being built here in Chinatown, and if that happens, some people would have to give up their property to make room for it. I don't want to risk losing my house to eminent domain."

I didn't quite follow all that, but I had to admit it was impressive that she, at her age, a Chinese American woman, was purchasing a house.

Anna May stroked the coverlet. "I'm sure you won't have any trouble selling this."

"Hopefully not." Ma refolded the blanket and wrapped her arms around it. "Come again to see us."

"I will. As soon as I can afford to furnish my new place."

Ma left, and I shifted on my feet. Anna May's kindness to Ma had mollified me, but I was still at a loss for what to say.

"Anyway," Anna May told me, "as I explained in my note, I knew the show meant so much to you, but I —"

"Note? What note?"

"I had notes delivered to the store right before the show. I sent one to that Mr. Haber, telling him off over what he did to you. And one to you explaining why I wasn't going to be there."

The tension inside me suddenly slackened. I'd thought Anna May had skipped the show because she didn't approve of James and me seeing each other. But she hadn't been signaling disapproval of *me*. She'd been trying to stand up for me!

"You didn't get the note?" Anna May said. "Of course you didn't! That bastard!" She practically spat the words. "I'm sorry, Ruby, but I just couldn't do it. I know you wanted to go through with the show for your own reasons. That's why I didn't back out earlier — so that Mr. Haber wouldn't have time to cancel the whole thing. But I was burning up over what he did to you. I couldn't pretend it didn't happen. I wanted to stick it to that lecherous frog."

*Couldn't pretend it didn't happen.*

"Did he blow his top?" Anna May smirked.

"He did. He blew, all right." I wasn't about to repeat what he'd said about her.

"But the show went on? How'd it go?"

"He told the audience you were sick. But it went on. It was fine." Even as I answered, my mind hopped to the argument I'd caused with her ba. I'd thought I was getting back at her for slighting me. Now I could see how screwy I'd been, how quick to jump to conclusions.

"Oh, Anna May, it was my fault that your ba went to see your movie. I encouraged him to see it. I knew he'd be appalled, but I was irked after everything that happened and . . . gosh, there's no excuse."

She raised her narrow, contoured eyebrows at me. "Well, I did want him to go."

"Still, I was being malicious, stirring things up between the two of you. I'm so sorry."

Anna May fluttered a breath between her lips. "I appreciate you saying so, but it's not your fault. That was far from our first go-round."

"I don't know what I was thinking," I said. "I guess I just wasn't at the time. I was so fired up when you said I wasn't good enough for James and then didn't turn up at the fashion show, and then I was fired —"

"Fired!"

I nodded.

Anna May cringed. "Oh, geez! Because I didn't show, right? Ruby, I'm sorry. That creep, he oughta . . ." She wrinkled her brow and cocked her head at me. "Wait a minute. I didn't say you weren't good enough for Jimmy. I said you weren't right for each other."

"Because he's off to college and I'm — I'm just . . ." I was at a loss for words. I didn't know what I was.

"Ruby!" Anna May stepped forward and reached across the desk to place a hand on my shoulder. "You're fine. You're great. And don't let anyone tell you any differently. But you'd told me about the break with that other boy, and I could see your heart was still in tatters."

The tears were threatening. She was being so kind to me. I couldn't believe I'd misunderstood her so completely.

"And Jimmy is . . . well, he's Jimmy. He's going to college like Papa wants him to.

"You seem to know everything that happens in the neighborhood," I said. "You knew that James Wong and I were seeing each other."

"Yes."

"Well, we aren't anymore. Someone told him about Russell." I waited for her to admit it. She blinked as if expecting me to say more. For a moment I began to doubt myself for suspecting her. Could someone else have seen Russell and me somewhere? Or maybe Russell had told one of his friends and somehow it had gotten to James? On the other hand, Mrs. Kuen wasn't offering any denials.

"Mrs. Kuen, you're the only person who knew about Russell."

She dropped her head briefly before she folded her arms and said, "Yes, I did talk to James. I felt it was my responsibility to let him know of your parents' intentions to match you with a suitable prospect, because it's not just *your* reputation that's at risk here."

I closed my eyes, expecting to feel a surge of anger. But strangely, a deep ache of disappointment sank into my bones.

"Why can't you understand that?" Her voice was laced with impatience. "It's your ba's business. Your brothers' futures! Our community. You've damaged our reputation, as well as my reputation and my connection to the Blythes' church because I introduced you to them."

I said nothing.

"The Chinese are always fighting for respectability in the eyes of the whites," she went on. "We've always had to do more to prove ourselves. You know the reputation of the district — fun houses, gambling, opium, exotic girls. They look at us and that's all they see."

"But is that really our fault? Our responsibility?"

Mrs. Kuen's perfect posture wilted. She sighed deeply. "It's not fair, but the white Americans run this country. We can't pretend what they think of us doesn't matter."

I pressed my lips against a rising swell of frustration. "So, what are we expected to do? Be only what they want us to be? Never step outside the limits they set for us? Make no mistakes?"

# 29

## MAY 1924

Back in the spring, seeing Russell and Aiko in the alley had done something to me that I couldn't explain. After they drove away that Friday afternoon, I made my way home and mechanically went through the motions of the weekend, pretending to do my homework and helping Ba in the store, but all the while, my mind was locked on Russell. I wished I'd never met him. Or Irene for that matter. If I hadn't been taking lessons from her, Russell wouldn't have noticed me.

I shouldn't have fallen for him. Never should've let him touch me.

But even as I fumed over those thoughts, another kind of heat ran through me. The scent of his skin, his hands sliding up my thighs, my chest near to bursting when he'd chased the streetcar shouting my name. I wanted to make him miss me. I wanted to forget him. Everything was tangled in my mind. But the worst part of it all was the bottled-up feelings with no release valve.

The Santa Anas whipped up that evening. A hot, dry wind blew in from the north, scattering the dirt from the unpaved streets and the railyard, carrying the faint scent of smoke from a distant wildfire. When Ma mentioned that my eyes were like steamed taro, swollen and purplish, I muttered that they were itchy from the dust blowing everywhere. But really it was the wreck inside me that was putting me in a daze.

Sleep eluded me that weekend, and by that Sunday night, long after everyone went to bed, I lay on my cot, sluggish and jumpy, with my covers tossed off. The wind whined in the street and stirred the moonlit curtains, which fluttered like flags of surrender. A train clattered down Alameda and shook the building. Then the train bells clanged, and something in me snapped.

I'd heard the same clanging every day, every night, since we'd moved to this city, but there was something so shrill, so rude in the sound that I bolted up in bed. We had grown used to the commotion of the trains passing right through our neighborhood, stepped aside to let the railcars pass, let them clatter and whistle through our dreams. We had become used to the indignity of the noise, the poor conditions, the second-class treatment. But no more.

I got out of bed then. Dressed and stole downstairs. Outside, the wind seethed in the alley as I scuttled to the street with the moon high in the sky to light the way. Shadows on the ground scampered alongside me. Rats, I was sure. But I wasn't bothered by them as I slipped up Alameda to Los Angeles Street, then Marchessault, then past the Plaza. I didn't know where I was going. Just that I wanted to get out. To go somewhere.

Then I was on the streetcar. The Red Car to Hollywood. It was very late. The only others in the car were the conductor, a couple sitting very close, and an old man nodding off. They paid no attention to me. I found a seat in the very back. The city flew by in a blur of glowing spots that the streetlamps cast on the sidewalks.

Fleeting whiffs of exhaust and smoke mixed with eucalyptus and oleander. I took it all in, inhaling the city, until we came to the open-air pavilion that was the Hollywood station.

I found myself walking north along the dark streets. The wind tugged at my skirts and seemed to propel me along. It rustled the branches of the blooming jacarandas. I knew the flowers to be purple, but in the night, they were black plumes overhead. There were few streetlamps here, spread far apart, but the hulking sign planted on the hill blinked brightly, first *HOLLY*, then *WOOD*, then *LAND*, before it started all over again. Russell had raved about that sign. Promised to take me to see it all lit up at night. Hadn't he?

The sign showed me the way, and it didn't take long to get there. Irene wanted to be close to the trolley, Russell had said, so she could run into the city any time she wanted. I stumbled through the half-landscaped lot to the back. I patted the ground under a large rock beside the door until I found the key. I hadn't truly expected it to still be in the same spot, but there it was, as if waiting for me.

My anger ran hot and cold — cold from wanting to freeze him out, but mostly hot with humiliation, rage, and frustration. The worst thing was that I had no way to reach him, to lay into him and tell him what I thought.

I unscrewed the flask and took another long swallow. The drink went down easier this time, so I took another, then lay there letting it steep in my body, loosening my nerves, my muscles. Another gust shook the trees outside. The shadows from their leaves flickered on the walls, and the metal hose of the sprayer head on its stand glinted near my shoes. I sat up, grabbed the sprayer, and gave the faucet a single turn. A thin stream rained into the tub and down the drain.

My lip twitched in amusement as I recalled Russell's shock when I'd turned the water on him. I gave the knob another twist, and the sprayer seemed to spring to life. I flicked it to make the stream ribbon and dance, but the water crept back toward me in the tub, so I climbed out. The gin had made me clumsy, and I dropped the sprayer head on the floor. I bent to turn the faucet off, but my head swam, and the faint shimmer of water on the tile seemed to wink at me. For a moment I studied my fingers, laced in the cross-handle knob. Then I twisted it hard. But not to turn it off.

The lines of water jumped and settled into a satisfying bow. Mesmerized, I watched it puddle on the floor. It was silvery in the moonlight, a spreading circle at first, but then the pool began to creep toward the door. Irene's voice sliced through my mind: *Get her out of here!*

I bit my lip until the metallic taste of blood was on my tongue. I wrenched the knob again, and again, until the valve was fully open. The water gushed out. For several minutes I did nothing as the water flowed into the hall, fanning over the oak floorboards, running toward the bedrooms and down the stairs.

Then I got out.

# 30

## JULY 1924

Now, in the alley beside the Lugo House, I jammed my fists into the patch pockets of my skirt and leaned against the building, no longer able to suppress the truth. Mrs. Kuen was right. I had been blocking it out. Pretending it hadn't happened. Denying that it mattered.

I stared up at the sun until it began to quiver before my eyes. I squeezed them closed, but the ghost of the sun was still there as a purplish splotch behind my lids.

I had been incredibly stupid. Not just the normal stupid of fooling around with a boy, the wrong boy, one who seduced me with attention and flattery but only saw me as an object, a toy. Being blinded by my own desire was bad enough, but then I had turned impetuous, reckless, vengeful. The truth was that my choices had a cost for me and for my family.

The five-dollar bill crumpled in the bottom of my pocket taunted me, goading me to get my photograph taken like Ba and Auntie Matchmaker wanted. Prospective husbands needed to examine me more closely. Ma had given up when she handed me that bill. She had tried, and I had tried, to save me from everything I didn't want, but mostly I'd been ignoring anything I wasn't willing to face up to.

That night in May, I had put the key back beneath the rock and hurried away from Irene's house. At the Red Car station, the lights were out, and I realized that the trolleys had probably stopped running for the night. I had no idea what time it was. The crescent moon had traveled east in the sky. It was strangely colored with a pinkish tinge. The wind's current swirled from one direction, then another. It seemed to be pushing me, urging me to go home. Home to Chinatown.

There was nothing to do but follow the tracks. I headed east on Hollywood to Sunset. It was desolate at this time of night, more so the farther east I traveled. The buildings and streetlamps became fewer and farther between. Tracts of undeveloped land opened to a distant darkness off one side of the road, and I suddenly felt alone and in the middle of nowhere.

The air was getting chilly. I was dimly aware of my shoes pinching, my toes and the backs of my heels rubbed raw. I had no sense of how long I walked before I realized I'd made it downtown. The density of the buildings comforted me. Spills of light from windows and streetlamps lit my way. I dipped into the shadows or crossed the street if I saw a loiterer on the sidewalk or partiers rolling out of a building. It was late by then, maybe close to dawn. Not many people, no more than a couple of vehicles. The city felt still and seemed to be all mine.

The wind died down, and a fog slowly rolled over the city, shrouding the streets, but I was on familiar ground, and I knew the way.

I reached Chinatown before daybreak, long after the late-night vice-seekers had stumbled out of the brothels and opium dens, but before the vegetable sellers had rolled out of bed.

Never had I been so glad to be home. I sneaked inside and collapsed into bed. I fell into a slumber so deep Ma couldn't rouse me that morning. She let me sleep through Monday, and for two days after that I skipped school and hid out in the library. And kept hiding out from the truth, even to myself.

But now I had to face up to what I had done.

I pulled my hand out of my pocket and bit at my thumb. The five-dollar bill was wadded in my fist, waiting for me to get my photograph taken.

*It's what you do next that matters.*

I smoothed out the bill and studied the image on the back, the turbulent landing of the settlers at Plymouth. Wind foamed the sea, rocked the boat, and whipped at their clothes as they strained to get ashore. I knew just how they felt.

the images appeared stiff and lifeless. Even if their souls weren't lost, they seemed to be horribly trapped on those prints.

I started to pull the door open when I noticed something else in the window — a placard on an easel. *A Special Inducement: One Dozen Beautiful Photographs $10.00.*

Ten dollars? I only had five. It wasn't nearly enough. I released a long breath that had been stuck in my chest. I'd been given a reprieve.

I turned to leave, but after a few steps, I stopped. If a dozen prints cost ten dollars, did that mean they would let me pay five dollars for six? I hated that the question had entered my mind, but there it was. Hadn't I resolved *to do what needs to be done*?

I dithered outside the barbershop next to the portrait studio, trying to unstick my feet and go back. The barbershop had its own poster in its window. *Bobbed Hair Has Come to Stay!* The sign featured headshots of women and children with variations of the cut. The photos were small because there were at least a dozen of them crammed on the poster, some of them overlapping to show both the front and the back of the style. But what struck me was how light and bright the models seemed compared to the heavy portraits right next door. With their unfettered necks and easy smiles, they looked so confident and happy.

A small placard was propped beside the poster. *We will bob your hair to suit your face! $5.00*

The long tail of my braid lay on my chest, thick and weighty as a chain. I recalled how Ma had styled my hair in that faux bob, how the air had grazed my neck.

Inside, the barber was shaving a man reclined in his chair. He saw me standing at the window and beckoned me to enter.

The five-dollar bill burned in my hand. A bob would mark me as an American and ensure that no old Chinese man would want me for a wife. What would Ba do then? What would I do?

The movie truck rattled behind me on the street, the backward lettering of *Metro Studio* flashing in its reflection in the shop window. I turned and watched the truck bear down the road, bumping and juddering as it hit the trolley tracks and wove around other vehicles. My eyes tracked it as it grew smaller and smaller in

I froze too. Part of me wanted to lay into him for judging me about things that were none of his business, but guilt skimmed the surface of my feelings, because everything between us had started with Ma's scheme.

"Hi, James," I said.

He began to drive the iron back and forth, the electric cord rasping against the hook it was strung through near the ceiling. "What are you doing here?"

His surliness almost had me turning on my heel. I doubted there was any chance for us now. Maybe Anna May was right that we weren't suited for each other. But for once, I didn't want to run from the situation.

"Listen, I know Mrs. Kuen told you that my ma and ba want me to get married. That's true, but I want you to know that I wasn't trying to trap you into anything."

His jaw tightened. He didn't slow the iron or look my way.

"I like you. I wasn't pretending about that. I didn't have any intention of getting married. To *anyone*, no matter how many guys my parents pushed on me."

He glanced up. "What do you mean you *didn't* have any intention of getting married? Have they found —"

"*Don't*," I clarified. "I *don't* have any intention of getting married." After speaking to Mrs. Kuen, I had almost relented, almost agreed to take the first step and have my picture taken. I had made mistakes, and the way forward *was* to do what was needed. But I had to do that on my own terms.

"Not anytime soon, anyway," I continued. "What happened before I met you had nothing to do with how I . . ." *Feel about you* or *felt about you*, I wasn't sure which to say. "Well, what was between us."

James put the iron on its stand. I had the sense that his mood had softened, but he didn't know how to respond. That was enough for now. If we were to go on in some fashion, much more would need to be said — more secrets shared, more difficulties hashed out. But now wasn't the time. He wasn't who I had come to see.

"Listen, is Anna May around?" I asked. "I need to ask her something."

He thrust his chin up toward the second floor. "She just got home. I'll go get her." He seemed glad to leave the room, but he turned up one side of his mouth before he went to the back.

I bounced on my toes as I waited for Anna May. When she came into the service area, I couldn't contain myself. "I'm so glad you're here! I had an idea and wanted to ask you a favor. A big one."

"Ruby!" Her eyes rounded. "Your hair! It's absolutely darling!"

"Thanks!" I primped it up and obligingly dipped and pivoted my head. "I just got it done. But listen, remember how you told me that sometimes film studios rent the props for the sets? And how your company is going to make pictures to highlight our culture? I want Chan's Art Emporium to be the exclusive supplier for Anna May Wong Productions."

Anna May tucked her lips between her teeth. Her shoulders dropped and she seemed to deflate right before my eyes.

"Well, maybe not exclusive, but at least throw us a little business?" I amended, worried I'd been too presumptuous.

"Of course, your store would be one of the first places I'd go to for props," she sighed. "But unfortunately, it seems Anna May Wong Productions is over before it even started."

"Over? What do you mean?"

She pressed her fingertips against her temples. "Creighton, the promoter my manager hired, turned out to be a rat. He's been using my name to borrow money and has racked up tons of debt under the production company. I just found out at that meeting I went to."

"That's terrible! How can he do that?"

Anna May shrugged.

I was floored by the vileness — and by the disappointment she must be feeling. "What are you going to do?"

"There's going to be legal wrangling. And I'll have to take whatever acting parts I can get until I've gotten everything straightened out." She raked her hands through her hair, then groaned.

"I'm so sorry. Is there anything I can do?" I had no idea how I could possibly help someone in her situation, but I own place. I've been decorating and I'd like a touch of chinoiserie."

Anna May and I exchanged the slightest of eye rolls. I placed the liuqin back on its hook.

"Well, if it's just the effect you're after, perhaps one of the pipas," I said to Miss Mathis. "These are very good pieces as well — not quite as special, but larger, so they would make a charming display on your wall."

Miss Mathis took a step back and studied the pieces. "Yes. I think they would be lovely in my library. I'll take all three of them and hang them on the wall over the piano."

Anna May clapped her hands. "June, I think that would be wonderful!" She winked at me.

"I agree. You have an excellent design sense, June." Frances came to stand beside us. "Ruby, your place is a true standout. I wish we had more time, but we really must get back to the studios. I've got a meeting this afternoon with the set designer."

Miss Mathis told me, "If you'll make up a bill of sale, I'll send someone over to deliver the payment and to pick up the pieces."

"Certainly." Marveling that Miss Mathis hadn't even asked about the prices, I went to the desk and pulled out the inventory book. As I scanned the pages and pages of items, Frances's mention of a meeting with the set designer echoed in my head.

I hurried to write up the ticket, and as I presented it to Miss Mathis, I turned to Frances. "Miss Marion, I was just remembering what you said at lunch that day in the commissary. About how rare it was to meet someone who wasn't champing at the bit to get in the pictures. Truth is, I've had a change of heart."

"Oh! Well, aren't you lucky to have a guide like Anna May to help you along. I'll bet she'll let you know when she hears about a little role for you."

I grinned at Anna May, whose eyebrows were pulled high on her forward. "I am lucky to have her help, but acting isn't what I'm interested in. It's the set design that intrigues me." I flung my arms out, gesturing to all the merchandise. "Here we've got all these lovely things that could be used in the backdrops of your scenes.

in my throat. "How I put my family in a difficult situation and hadn't wanted to admit that."

She'd lifted the cup to her lips but now brought it down without taking a sip. I had her attention.

"You were right about that," I said. "I wanted to pretend nothing had happened, and I didn't want to believe what I'd done could haunt the business or our reputation."

The expression on her face told me she was wary of my deference. She glanced at Mr. Lew, who was listening with obvious curiosity. I wasn't sure how much he knew, but I was pretty certain he was too dignified to pry.

"My mistakes can't be undone," I continued, "and maybe people will find out about them, but I — *we* aren't really improving our station if we're always trying to make ourselves into what other people want or to behave the way they think we should."

Mrs. Kuen pursed her lips.

"Maybe I'll fail miserably in the end, but I *am* doing what needs to be done." I gestured to the store, the displays I'd arranged, the crowd that I'd invited. "Which is doing what moves my heart."

Mr. Lew closed his eyes for a fraction of a second, an almost imperceptible nod of encouragement. Mrs. Kuen gazed into her cup, jiggling it to swirl the tea. Much as I had always tried to disregard what she said, in truth I wanted her support now, because the community did matter to me. But if that support didn't materialize, I'd still find my way.

After a long moment, she took a sip of tea, then inclined her head to Mr. Lew and me. "The event is certainly well attended."

I drew in a large breath. Like when I'd gotten my braid cut off, a weight I hadn't realized was there fell away. "I'm hoping this open house will help Ba recover the money he lost on my account. Maybe it'll bring more business to the community. Did Mr. Lew explain that our goal is mostly to make contacts tonight? Though I wonder, have we made any sales, Mr. Lew?"

Mr. Lew picked up the ledger and showed me a stack of receipts beneath it. Most of those sales were probably for the usual bric-a-brac and curios the scenarioists happened with the Blythes. But surely all my work had made an impression on him.

My gaze went back to Mrs. Kuen. She was trying to help me, offering both Ba and me the simplest solution. If I went back to school, I'd do my last year, maybe work in the store in the afternoons like I had in the past. But wouldn't that be going backward, back to being merely an obedient Chinese daughter? I could never be that again.

Still, I didn't want to be cast out of the family, out of the community. I wanted to build a place for myself here. I sneaked another sideways glimpse at Ba. "A business class? Really?" Maybe going back to school could give me a fresh start with Ba. I would happily get my diploma if he would give up the idea of my getting married. "And Lincoln High is where most of the Chinatown kids go, isn't it?" I asked Mrs. Kuen.

"Yes, that's right. I understand some of the girls want to start a civic club. One of them heard about a young women's group called the Square and Circle Club starting up in San Francisco's Chinatown. A girls' equivalent to the Chinese American Citizens' Alliance."

My mind wheeled back to my old friends in San Francisco. This sounded like the sort of thing they might get involved in. I missed them. I missed having a pack.

"I suppose it will be nice for you to get back in school and make some young friends after a summer such as this one. It's been so" — she turned to Ba and blinked at him meaningfully — "uneventful."

She was telling him that the gossip about me had not caught fire, that my reputation was intact.

"Except, of course, everything you've done to promote the shop. You've shown quite the talent for this work." The corners of her mouth tipped up into a smile. "School starts in another week. I could go with you to get registered." She turned to Ba. "I can come for her around ten." It was half statement, half question. I supposed even Mrs. Kuen knew her influence could only go so far.

Ba kept his head down for the longest time, so long that Mrs. Kuen's smile began to fade and a panicky feeling grew inside me. But then he drew in a short breath and heaved it out. It was a sigh of acquiescence, and my heart surged even before he straightened up and gave a tense nod. "You can do the books after school and work the floor here on Saturdays and Sundays."

I was bursting with relief, too overwhelmed to say anything. He wasn't just walking back from the marriage scheme — he was giving me his blessing to work in the store again. This was his way of forgiving me, accepting me.

Mrs. Kuen started placing the used teacups on a tray. "Is your ma in the back?" she asked. "I'll take these since I'm going to speak to her."

Ba and I watched as she maneuvered through the thinning crowd until she passed into the back.

It wouldn't hurt to go back to school and graduate. In fact, I even found myself looking forward to it. The club did sound interesting and maybe I could make some friends.

I turned to Ba. The strain of his long journey showed on his face. He had been uncharacteristically leaden and sluggish all evening. For the first time all night, it hit me that he'd traveled halfway around the world and back. In a way, I felt like I had done the same this summer.

"Ba, you sent us some lovely pieces. We sold a few of them tonight, the huanghuali trestle-leg table and two rosewood trunks . . ."

"Good, good." He nodded and his gaze wandered over my head. I glanced behind me at Ma's quilt, the cranes flying up to the gold-threaded sun she had added. *Ambition.*

"You arranged everything nicely," he said.

I shot him a smile, agreeing that it had turned out well in the end.

Jones, the Gravesend Writers, and Rebecca Petruck, who advised me on an early draft. And I'm so especially grateful to the people who helped me track down articles, resources, and pieces of information, including librarians Mary McCoy, Kelly C. Wallace, and Alice Schock from the Los Angeles Public Library system; Marie Concannon from the University of Missouri Library; Li Wei Yang from the Huntington Library; Christopher Salvano and Matthew Barrett from the LA County Metro Transportation Authority Library and Archive; and biographer Katie Gee Salisbury.

The employees of Thorndike Press hope you have enjoyed this Large Print book. All our Thorndike Large Print titles are designed for easy reading, and all our books are made to last. Other Thorndike Press Large Print books are available at your library, through selected bookstores, or directly from us.

For information about titles, please visit our website at https://www.gale.com/thorndike.